# PERFUME RIVER

### A NOVEL

## KATHLEEN PATRICK

*For my family, again, because... well, love.*

# CONTENTS

# PRELUDE

I was twelve. It was spring. I sat at Gran's knee on the screened-in porch, making potholders out of pink and lime green polyester loops. Over. Under. Over again. I arrived that morning with two suitcases, a box of books, the stuffed panda I'd had since I was four, my radio, and my pillow.

My parents agreed that a time apart was a good idea. Maybe for the summer. A separation. My parents and I were separated. The summer turned into an entire year, my seventh-grade year, but I'm getting ahead of myself.

The oboe. I was living with Gran in her farmhouse outside St. Cloud, six miles from my own home. My parent's home. She gave me the back bedroom with roses on the wallpaper and a pink chenille bedspread. The house was old and comfortable. It smelled like talcum powder and coffee. Everything was in the same place it had been the last time I was at Gran's house, except she cleared drawers in the bedroom and gave me a shelf in the bathroom for my toothbrush and things. She did this on short notice. After a couple of hours, Gran integrated me into her life without thinking twice. I had changed lives because of the oboe, or so I thought.

My mother and father usually said too much when they were fighting, and they were usually fighting. On this particular occasion, they fought about me. At least that is my memory of the event. I can recall where many fights began. The physical origins: in front of the refrigerator, on the back steps as we headed down to the Mississippi for a boat ride, on the way home from my sister Allison's high school graduation.

The first comment, which received the first glare, which led to the first angry words. This time, they stood in the front hall by the desk. I got my way too much. I was spoiled. She spoiled me. He ignored me. He never wanted me to do anything. I was too quiet. I was too loud. I never practiced that damn oboe they bought for me. I practiced right next to the TV room. I was a schemer. The light bill needed to be paid. She forgot to pay the bills. He forgot her birthday. I forgot to tell them when I left the house.

Gran brushed the top of my head with her strong, large hand. "So tell me."

"Tell you what?"

"About the oboe."

I wanted to tell her how I wished I could control things and make it all right again. I thought I could fix things up if only given a chance. I wanted to talk and talk until none of it remained inside of me. Gran was like that. I could tell her about the littlest dream, one that was even confusing and parts were left out, and she would lean forward and listen to my every word. She would say what happened then? Were you surprised? Did anything happen after that? And if it did, if there was more, I would draw out the details like a fine sketch, highlighting the facial features, explaining the layout of the room, describing every item of clothing I wore, everything that I did and remembered, and it would all be important to her. I loved her for it.

"I threw it into the river."

"Why?" She ran her fingers down the long dark braid of my hair.

"1 don't know. It cost a lot of money. It was important to me." We sat not talking for a long time. "I'm supposed to play in the spring band concert next Friday."

A robin anxiously hopped around the front yard, seeking bits of straw for her new home. "I don't know why I did it."

"It's not your fault, Sam. Don't try to figure it out. Your parents are the ones who need to sort out their lives. You're staying here. You're safe. We will deal with this."

I tied off the end of a potholder, making a small loop to hang it on one of the magnet hooks on Gran's refrigerator.

"Let's go for a walk," Gran said. "Get our noses sunburned. Get some exercise."

"I don't know. They kept yelling and saying the same things over and over again. I couldn't listen anymore. I took the backstairs down to the dock; I still had my horn. I remember what it felt like, the cold metal keys, my fingers, the wood. Then I just closed my eyes and threw it into the river. My oboe. In the river."

Years later, I look back and still remember the energy springing out of my arms with that instrument. When I opened my eyes, the oboe bobbed on the brown current. A weird wooden fish floating down to New Orleans. A musical cry for help. A life raft.

# 1
___

S o it wasn't in the cards. Sam tossed the form letter onto the floor next to her. Grants and rejections. She was used to it. Still, it would have meant she could quit her job at the frame shop and work on her art full time, even rent a studio downtown with enormous windows and light streaming in on her in the early morning. Winter sun warming the place, spilling over into her life, filling up all the cracks. And there were cracks, small crevices wearing away her resistance; she wasn't as good at rejection as she used to be. Then she would shrug her shoulders and say it was their loss, his loss, anybody's loss but hers. Now it felt like what it was, a missed opportunity to get on with her life the way she had envisioned it as a working artist with a few shows and occasional sales, some teaching, and freelance commercial work to get her through. Now it felt lonely, depressing. Another out. Another inning.

She stretched out on the wood floor, her slim body in sweatpants and an old Jimmy Carter T-shirt. Samantha Ellings is not a loser, she thought to herself. I don't give up that easily. I'll try again. It only takes one show, one grant, one shot of good luck.

Familiar territory. She felt the blues and then talked herself out of them. Life had always been that way. If you wanted to stay sane, you kept things to yourself and your eye on the horizon. Today she didn't believe it herself, but no matter, she had the day off. Perhaps she wouldn't be looking at the world as if it were exploding in color, but she'd go see Netty, ride her bike without using her hands, steer with her keen sense of balance, and keep things under control.

"I STILL SAY you should run along and spend this nice day with some young man." Netty shuffled the cards again. She sat in a wicker rocker on the other side of their TV tray table.

Sam sat in stocking feet on the bed. "Why are you so eager to get rid of me? I don't remember saying I was looking for male companionship. Just give it a rest, Netty. Let's go. Am I winning?"

"Not a chance, dear. Not a chance."

The cottonwood tree on the boulevard in front of ChoiceCare dropped seed tufts onto the street and sidewalk below. Netty had been Gran's best friend. Her son opened a video store in Minneapolis and made the move from St. Cloud four years ago. Netty made the move last year, after they sold the farm. "I remember when you were wearing braces." Netty laughed. "Your Gran always said you'd be the best-looking girl in Stearns county when they took the barbed wire off your teeth."

"She said that?" Sam smiled. "Then she told me not to be vain and worry about some little wires that couldn't hide a smile like mine. Gran was a double-talker if I ever saw one. Barbed wire."

Netty held the deck of cards to her lips as a smile spread out from both sides. Her hands trembled, the blue rivers of blood showing through parchment skin. "She would like to see us playing cards together like this. Passing a quiet day in the city."

"I'm sure she would like to see me win," Sam said. "I was her favorite, you know. Now deal out that deck; I feel lucky."

## 2

"So I told him if he would not pay me for the photographs, they would not be hanging on his wall anymore. I put them under my arm and walked out. Just like that." Gary finished his drink. The bar reeked of beer and stale smoke.

Sam gathered her thick hair up off her neck and twisted it into a bun, smiling at Gary. "God, it's hot. Should we get out of here?"

She wanted to listen to his voice, to talk and listen to her own voice, to hear the two of them all night saying important things, saying unimportant things, whispering away from people and bar popcorn. She didn't want to be alone.

Gary drove around Lake Calhoun. Sam leaned back in her seat. Spotlights poured across the groomed lawns of huge, old-money houses. "Want to come over for a drink?" Gary asked. She shook her head yes, still eyeing the pillars and bay windows. It was a beautiful night. Too early to sleep.

Sam stood in the dark living room of the small rambler with a glass of wine; Gary lit a candle and turned on the stereo. The walls evaporated into shadow as they danced, her shoulder fitting into the curve of his. Sam's thighs leaned into his as she listened to the slow jazz melody. She let herself get lost in his arms, in the musical dark, throwing off every argument, every defense.

Gary took her hand and led her down the hall to the bedroom. She knew this part. They undressed in the half-light from the street lamp and lay down on the waterbed. The bed's small waves followed the desire.

Later, listening to Gary's steady breathing, Sam stared at the ceiling. Pale boxed light shown in from the window. It was always this way. Allowing her body to surrender to the passion, and then later, distrusting her feelings, trying to make sense of it. She had been in love once. It felt like slick ice on the freeway; the car going into a fast skid. The skid wasn't painful, but the knowledge of the inevitable impact was, and she'd been right. Face first into a brick wall.

She closed her eyes. She would always be working on that one, trying to figure it out. How can you live your life in any kind of rhythm and still be open to love? One thing was certain: she wasn't in love now. Gary was a nice guy. She'd wanted it to work, but she didn't love him. They were just friends. You don't make love with friends, Sam thought, so what am I doing here?

The long dock slipped into the Mississippi behind her house, stretching out into the thick autumn mist. Sam still couldn't see the end as she walked along the weathered boards. Too much fog. But each foot followed the other, as she obeyed some sleepy need to move forward. A gaping hole left by three missing boards caused her to pause before jumping over the expanse of dark water. She glanced back and saw the floating bodies again, as if for the first time, human bodies suspended on the waves like stiff plaster mannequins.

Sam jumped back across the open water and ran toward the shore, but as it happened every other time, the beach was no longer visible. The wooden planks stretched out endlessly both ways. She attempted to scream, but nothing escaped from her throat. Gasping, she heard the faint tinkling of a bell beyond the slapping waves. The outline of a small rowboat became clearer in the gray cloudiness. Someone was calling her name. The distant voice sounded like her mother. Then she saw what looked like her father, holding her mother's head on a platter.

Sam tossed in her sleep, wrapped in the familiar skin of the nightmare. She forced her eyes back to the water, knowing the bodies would be gone, and they were. In their place, huge water lilies bloomed in a calm river. Pastel flowers the size of beach balls crowded both sides of the dock. An overpowering sweetness filled her lungs until she was certain it would choke her.

Sam sat up in bed and searched for the comfort of her bedroom in the late night. A hatrack hung over the dresser. A straight-backed chair stood draped with layers of clothes. A couple camera tripods. The door on the wrong wall. She rolled over slowly and smelled someone else's sheets, another body beneath the covers. She closed her eyes again, backtracking to dinner, to the bar and dancing, to Gary's careful hands on her shoulders, the pleasant rhythm of sexual patterns: his lips sliding behind her ear, her hands finding the curve of his back, the distance one can acquire in the dark. While they made love, she ran out ahead of herself, listening to distant breathing.

She didn't even know Gary's address. They'd dated off and on for a few months, but she didn't remember the name of the street outside the bedroom. The evening floated over her like so many others. Details. She tried to sleep. In the morning, she would go home.

Gary stood bare-chested at the stove, spooning brown crystals into a cup. "Coffee? I'm out of the real stuff." He was intensely handsome. Curly auburn hair. Cheekbones Sam wanted to follow with her fingers. Walnut eyes.

"Thanks." Gray formica table, piled high with newspapers. White walls. Breadcrumbs by the toaster. The disturbing dream stayed out at the edge of her vision, blurry and indistinct. She drank the bitter coffee and stared out the window as Gary got ready for work at Rolens Ad Agency. The familiar silent gap.

He clicked on the radio and read the comics while he tied his tie. The scene was a rerun. Sam delighted in the tenderness, listening to words that could tip an iceberg on its side. She relished all that emotion, but in the morning she understood the rules. Don't take it too seriously. Don't ask too much. Don't tie knots. She always returned home, noticing the vibrant colors of the trees lining the boulevard; colors so vital she could cry. Brilliant ocher and gold splashed against the empty, consistent blue.

"Want a ride home or to work? I've got plenty of time."

Sam forced a smile. "Yeah, home would be good. I've got the day off. I might sketch at the bus stop." She stood up and stretched, pulling the sleeves of her sweater down over her hands.

Sam put on dark sunglasses as they stepped out into the bright morning. The lawn was thick and long. "Who does your yard work?" she asked.

Gary sighed. "Next weekend."

Sam glanced down at the corner before getting into the car. The street sign read Van Buren and Fifth.

## 3
_____

number 17 would come by soon, Sam thought. She found a spot near the corner and put down her canvas bag and drawing paper. She used her coat as a pillow and sat down, resting against the wall of the doughnut shop. A mopish looking dog sat in the middle of the sidewalk, attending to fleas on his hind flank, turning himself in circles, trying to reach his back.

As the red metro bus approached, Sam pulled out a pencil and propped her drawing pad on her knees. The sun was out, playing up the autumn colors. Reaching into her bag, she pulled out a Walkman and headphones. The bus pulled away from the curb, leaving its fumes and several riders. She sketched one man's face, his mustache like a caterpillar crawling over his top lip. "So much trouble in the world," she sang softly to herself as people milled about, stepping off the curb and looking further down Nicollet Avenue for the next approaching bus. An older man in a black knee-length coat and plain trousers stood reading the Minneapolis Star and Tribune, shifting his weight from one leg to the other each time he turned a page. A few riders wandered off in other directions. "So much trouble in the world." A man in a gray flannel suit and oxfords was lighting up a cigarette when the dog came up and sniffed at his heels.

"Get lost, mutt. Go on. Go home."

The thin dog drew its tail between its legs and sulked off. A slight breeze caught the smoke from the cigarette and pulled it toward the open street. A young Black boy, ten or eleven, walked down the sidewalk, his head facing the cement, as if studying its cracks and divisions. He wore jeans and high-tops, the laces undone, with knots at the ends. Oblivious to Sam, he walked past her, his hands pushed deep into his jacket pockets. He turned the corner before she saw his face.

One woman, wearing a uniform, walked toward Bayfield's doughnut shop. "Afternoon," Sam said. "Going to work?" The woman smiled halfheartedly and walked into the shop. Sam shrugged and finished the sketch of the man with the mustache while noting the leaves in the gutter near the street, the empty Pepsi can laying outside the waste bin, the dog headed into the alley across the street.

She tried to concentrate on the details, but the night before crowded her thoughts. That dream again. And Gary. What was she going to do about him?

Sam noticed the young boy was coming back down the sidewalk, his head facing the cement, but she could see the deep caramel color of his skin, his curly black hair, and the turned-up collar of his jacket. As he got closer, she pulled off her headphones. "Hi." Sam smiled. He walked past, barely glancing at her, his face registering no emotion.

Sam turned to her sketchpad, "Long jaw bone. Long, long scarf. Lady, who does your hair?" Sam shook her head as she perused the crowd, then looked at her sketchpad. "Turn this way, please. Yes, yes. Very nice."

When the boy in the tan jacket approached again, Sam spoke. "You're awful serious. Lighten up. It can't be that bad." He leaned against the brick wall near her. The tops of his jeans were tucked inside high-top Adidas. Sam kept mumbling, "Umm. Some profile, mam. Yes. Have a chair, very good."

Soon the bus pulled away from the curb, leaving the stop empty. Sam looked around her. The boy slid down to a sitting position. It was almost four o'clock. The sun was backing off a bit and the air cooling. "You lost?"

He shot a glance over at Sam. "Shut up, lady."

"Sorry. I was just kidding." Sam noticed his tense

shoulders, remembering the feeling. "My name is Sam. Samantha Ellings."

"Who cares?" he said, half to himself as he stood up and pushed his hands into the pockets of his jacket, stretching the cloth. He walked away, turned the corner, and disappeared.

# 4

Late Tuesday afternoon, Sam was back at the bus stop sketching. The boy surprised her. He stood over the paper. "Why you hanging around here?"

Sam shrugged. "I like it here. Why are you hanging around here?"

The boy backed away. "You're weird."

"No. I'm Sam." She could tell he'd been crying. "Hey. You want a doughnut? I'm buying."

"Funny lady."

"No. Serious business."

He hesitated. "I've got money, and I don't eat with weirdos."

"I'm no weirdo."

"Well, you're strange, and I don't talk to strangers sitting on the sidewalk like they got no place to go."

"Good point. That's smart. But we have met, and I told you my name and I've drawn your Adidas five times."

"Ha." The boy walked over to the waste bin and began kicking at the Pepsi can on the ground. "Right lady."

"I have. Look." She held up the sketch pad and flipped through a few of the pages. He kicked the can over near her, glancing at the sketches.

"They ain't too bad. But you are strange." He stood over Sam, looking at her drawing pad.

"Why are you walking in circles?" she asked.

"Why are you drawing?"

"Because I can't find anyone who'll eat doughnuts with me!" She held up her shoulders, as if the answer were simple. He picked up the pop can and threw it over near the trash bin.

"I'll buy my own," he said.

"Okay. Deal. But can I give you my money so I don't have to leave all my stuff?" Sam asked. He nodded, looking annoyed by the whole thing. Sam held out the five. "I want two chocolate covered and a powdered. I've got some Gatorade, if you want some of that."

"Nope. I don't drink with weirdos." He took the money and walked inside.

She spread her coat out on the cement, an old green army jacket, oversized and filled with buttons from rock bands and political campaigns. Sam motioned for the boy to have a seat. "I should know your name, I mean, sharing my jacket and all."

He stood over her, the bag of doughnuts in his hand. "I don't need to sit there. The sidewalk is okay."

"So is the middle of the street, but I'd rather you just sit down and stop making a big deal out of it. Besides, I'm hungry. You sure you don't want some Gatorade? It's good."

"Rexel."

"What?" Sam asked.

"Rexel Henry Johnson."

"Well, I'm pleased to make your acquaintance, Rexel."

Samantha smiled and waved at the jacket. He sat down and passed the bag and change to her. "Three chocolate covered, the third's yours, I take it?"

"Yeah. And I paid the 35 cents. Your change is all there."

"Well, it better be." Sam raised her eyebrows.

"Three doughnuts is a lot. How come you ain't fat?"

"I missed lunch today," she said with her mouth full. "Pretty good, huh?"

"You live around here?" Rexel asked.

"Yeah. You?"

"Why you hanging out here?"

"I like to draw people waiting around. Decided I'd try

a new area. Good background across the street."

"It's stupid to draw bus stops." Rexel looked off in the other direction, finishing his doughnut.

"Well now, have you ever tried it, Rexel Harry Johnson?"

"Henry, not Harry." He looked disgusted. "Harry's a dog's name."

"Nope. Alexander's a dog's name. Alex for short."

"You got a dog?" He turned to face her.

"Yeah. You like dogs?"

He shrugged. "They're okay. Your dog named Alex?"

"Maybe," Sam smiled, starting a second doughnut.

"What kind is it?" He leaned closer.

"A Sheltie. He looks like a little collie. He's a good size for the house, and I have a backyard at my place. He plays out there when I'm—"

"What's the music?" Rexel motioned to the Walkman.

"Bob Marley and the Wailers. Survival. Kaya. Selected Best."

"Ain't he Black?" Rexel brushed pebbles from the area where the sidewalk connected with the brick of the doughnut shop facade.

"Last time I checked, why?"

Rexel shrugged. "I just thought so."

"You like reggae?" With the word "reggae," Sam moved her head and shoulders, as if dancing.

"Nah. I doubt it."

Sam wiped her mouth with the sleeve of her sweatshirt. "I see. Well, I like it. Such positive vibrations," she said in a singsong voice.

"Funny."

"Real funny. You're pretty funny, Rexel Henry Johnson."

He stood up to leave. Dusted the crumbs from his jeans. "Yeah. See you around."

"Yeah. I'll be drawing here awhile. Stop by and circle the block anytime." Rexel was already walking off as she called after him, "Thanks for the company, Rexel!" He waved a hand behind him, not turning around.

Noting some textures of the buildings in the background of her first sketch, Sam wrote a couple of things on the edge of the paper for later finishing work. The sun settled behind the warehouse across the street, making it difficult to work.

She packed up her supplies and stood up, stretching her back and long arms, taking stock of the subject matter. A stocking cap with a Vikings patch. Worn tennis shoes over pink and green socks. Black and white spiked hair. The passengers were guppies, she thought, swarming along the surface of a square world of water. The scene wasn't inherently interesting. Perhaps she was wasting her time. The dog needed water, and she had a night class at the Art Institute. Sam boarded the bus, found an empty seat, and pulled on her headphones.

## 5
---

At work, leaning over the table, Sam arranged the cranberry and steel double mat on the photo. She turned up the radio just as her boss walked in from the front reception area.

"That's loud enough, Sam. People out front might think we're running a dance studio back here. What are you listening to, anyway?"

"Progressive jazz-funk-rock. Heard of it? Therapy for the soul, Bart. Pure medicine."

Bart smiled. "Yeah, well, keep it down."

Sam dialed the telephone, cradling the receiver on her shoulder. "Leah Thomas, please," Leah worked publicity at the Guthrie theater. She and Sam grew up together. They were roommates for the first three years of college, then Sam studied in England and Leah moved in with Darin.

"Hi, Lee. It's me. Want to have lunch?"

"Are we talking brown bag in Loring Park or sit down, run up a tab?"

"Sit down. Small tab," Sam replied. "I just want to talk. How about 12:30 at the Champion?"

"Sounds good."

"Now get back to work," Sam said. "Time is money."

"Darin got promoted at IDS." Leah dipped a piece of fresh broccoli into the dill dip. "Pretty good bucks too. We might get another apartment with more room and garage parking. I'm not looking forward to winter. There's never any place to park the damn car; it would be great to have it inside."

"Yeah, I feel the same way about my bike." Sam smiled. "It's hell trying to parallel park that thing when they haven't plowed."

"Since we're discussing the starving artist, how is your work coming? Do you have anything new I haven't seen?"

"Nothing finished. I'm working on three pieces, all elderly women posed at the bus stop. We're doing some work in watercolor in my class at the Institute. I may try these in watercolor, just to see what happens. But I'm trying to get a show going for spring somewhere. Who knows? How's Darin these days? Has he been behaving for a change?"

"Ah, Sam. He's not a bad guy. I know you don't think Darin's right for me. Well, I suppose you think that sometimes, but things are okay now." Leah sighed and looked down at the twisted napkin in her hands.

"Well, I haven't forgiven him for that shitty trick with the data processor, but I guess if you say it's okay, I'll ease up. It's not that I don't like him so much, it's that I care about you. And he better watch it, that's all."

"Have you seen Gary lately?" Leah lifted the fine blond hair off her neck.

"Who? Oh yeah, him. Off and on. He's in Canada this week on a shoot." Sam played with the carnation in the center of the table.

"And?"

"And nothing. I don't miss him. I'll see him when he gets back. Romantic, huh?"

"Utterly." Leah paused. "You need a new man in your life."

"I need another cup of coffee. I need a new toaster oven, but I do not need a new man. I'm pretty sure I'm destined to failure in that department. Fated to a lonely life. Sigh. Oh, but I met a nice little kid. Well, nice isn't the right word. Rather a smartass, but I like him."

"God, this sounds bad. You are talking about serious problems here, Samantha. Stay away from little boys."

"Oh, Leah, get serious. He's just a kid. We're buddies, sort of. He's been hanging around the bus stop where I'm drawing and giving me a hard time. Seems like he's got lots of time to kill."

"1 don't believe this conversation right now," Leah said.

"It's okay to have young friends, isn't it? I get a kick out of him. He's got the most intense brown eyes you can imagine and what an attitude; something's bugging him."

"Samantha... "

"I don't think he has many friends. I might adopt him."

"Sure. Why not? Sam's Social Services, in action." Leah motioned for the check.

Sam dug in the pocket of her faded Levis, pulling out a couple of crumpled bills. "Leah, can you catch the tip? I'm kind of low."

"Sure," Leah said. "By the way, I can get you a couple of comps to the new show at the theater, if you're interested."

"Great," Sam said. "I'll talk to Gary about it next week and call you."

As she walked to the gallery, Sam thought about Friday. It was her day off. She could handle work one more day, and then a three-day weekend. Gary would still be in Toronto, photographing airplanes and Canadian sunsets for his tourism layout.

Sam looked around while waiting for the light. People were wearing heavier coats. The fall was settling in. She wouldn't have many pleasant weeks of outdoor drawing left. Then she'd have to bribe the manager of Bayfields doughnut shop to let her have a table by the window when it wasn't busy. Sometimes she actually attracted people. Folks interested in looking at her work, trying to find their faces in the lines of people bundled up, scarves over their mouths, eyes just above the bulk. Everyone waiting for the next bus, hoping it would come soon.

THE LAST TIME she'd been to the Guthrie theater, she'd gone with Eric. She wore the old tuxedo she found at a secondhand shop, rolled up the sleeves, and wore a beautiful silky white blouse underneath. She felt pretty. Rhinestone earrings dangling down to her shoulders, playing in the thick brunette curls. Manicured nails.

Eric wore a dinner jacket and looked like he was waiting for an airplane, his face distracted and furtive. After the show, in Carlyle's restaurant downtown, over a drink, he turned to Sam and announced that he and his old girlfriend had worked things out. "I didn't know how to say this. When to tell you. This isn't easy for me. If I'd met you at some other time. But we're going to do it. Get married, I mean. Start a family, probably. Shit. I think it's what I want." He said it all in one gasping breath, drinking the whiskey down in gulps afterward. Sam sat looking at her hands on the table, long, slim fingers intertwined, budding red on each nail, and listened. All eyes. All ears. He said they were going to get a house in the suburbs. He was starting with a young computer firm. Lots of promise.

Samantha looked around at the people at the bar. The velvet, the wool, and silk blends, the gold. Everyone wanted to be on stage that night. All sipping wine and brandy and discussing Chekov. It was too much. "Eric," her voice sounded steady. "Great! I'm glad to hear you've made plans. It sounds like you thought this one out. Of course, I had no idea, but then I wasn't the one thinking about it, was I? But I'm glad for you. Ecstatic, actually. Now, I have to powder my nose. Will you be a dear and order me one more glass of wine? I'll only be a minute."

Sam left Eric with his mouth open. She headed to the back of the lounge, noting the brass trim, the oak bar. Forest green upholstery. Images for later, shapes and colors to occupy blank canvas. The texture of the feelings to go along with the moment. The colors of the north woods.

She stepped out the back door and the cool evening breeze hit her. The bastard. She walked down Nicollet Mall; the night air smelled of early spring. A calm wave of heat near the end of February melted the ice off the sidewalks to remind everyone that the weather would change if they were patient.

The next day, she gave the tuxedo to Leah and called up Gary Hamlin to see if he'd like to get together again. They visited the zoo and took pictures of the animals with their furry winter coats. Shaggy, thick pelts harboring them from the cold. Hay and corn scattered on the snow. At the zoo, Sam had an odd image of Eric in a cage, behind fences of steel and barbed wire, his face criss-crossed with metal boundaries.

## 6

After untying the bandana around the right leg of her jeans, Sam rang the buzzer. She grabbed the door, maneuvered her bike in through the cramped entryway and up the flight of stairs to her best friend's apartment. The hallway reeked of spaghetti sauce and stale cigarettes.

"So he's getting it somewhere else. Big deal." Leah held the door open. "We're not married, right? It is the eighties, after all."

Sam leaned her ten speed against the living room wall. Leah smelled like booze. It wasn't a surprise. "Tell me the whole thing." She sat down on the couch and pulled off her hooded sweatshirt.

Leah shrugged. "Simple. Darin didn't come home last night. At ten o'clock this morning, I get a call. He says he got drunk, stayed at a buddy's house. Then this woman gets on the other line. You know, not knowing anyone was using the phone, and when she hears him talking says, 'Sorry, Darry.' I mean, Jesus. Darry? He says it's the guy's wife. Yeah, right. And he'll be home after some meeting at his office."

"And is that when you started drinking?" Sam looked at the clock. It was one-fifteen.

"Don't start on me, Sam. Didn't you hear a word I said?"

"Sure, and I want to talk about it. Let's go for a walk and get some air."

Leah perched on the arm of an easy chair facing Sam. "Have I ever told you that you smile at some of the worst times? Have I?" She flashed a fake smile, lifting her chin high.

Sam looked at her fingernails. "Yeah, once or twice."

"You're so damn happy all the time."

"Look. I didn't come over here for this. I understand you're mad at Darin, but don't take it out on me. If I smile at the wrong time, I'm sorry. I came over because you called and asked me to." Sam turned toward the window and twisted a strand of hair around her finger.

Leah poured something down the sink. The two women had a history. They grew up together. They learned how to smooth over rough edges. And they both had seen rough edges. Sam turned around and said, "How about some scrambled eggs? I'll make you some tea and you can take a quick shower. I'll even squeeze some orange juice."

"Help yourself! Betty Crocker. So I need a shower, huh?"

"It couldn't hurt. It might give you a lift." Sam headed for the refrigerator.

"Some lift. If he comes in, keep him here. I have a few questions for him."

Sam began cooking out of habit. If someone is upset, you give them some food and hot coffee. You listen and apologize for them. Don't worry, Mom, it didn't wreck anything. I can sew it back together. The shirt wasn't that great, anyway. See Dad, you didn't hurt her. She'll be okay, won't you Mom? Come on, I'll call Gran and tell her it's still okay to come over. It's all right. I'm okay.

"FEELING BETTER?" Sam asked.

"Define that." Leah wrapped a towel around her wet hair.

Sam sat on the kitchen counter, eating a piece of toast. "Well, it's possible it was a wife. You should at least hear him out."

"But Darry? What about that?"

"What if she didn't know his name?"

"And if he's lying to me?"

"Move out."

Leah used her fork to push the eggs around on her plate. "Would you?"

Sam turned the water faucet on and pulled out the rinse hose, spraying the dirty dishes in the sink. "I think so. I don't know. I mean, when I first started seeing Eric, he was still seeing what's-her-name. And sometimes I thought about him lying to me when he said it was over between them." She paused. "It always sounds easier when it isn't you."

Leah dumped the cold eggs down the disposal and patted Sam on the shoulder. "Thanks for the protein, lady. I feel better already. I suppose he'll be crawling in any time."

Sam jumped down from the counter. "I'm riding over to the Art Institute to look at a new show. Call if you want to talk. I'll be home by six o'clock."

"Forgive me if I forgive him?"

"Yeah. Just let him know he doesn't deserve it."


A CHILLY WIND snaked in around the neck of her sweatshirt as Sam rode towards the museum. The gusts brought dead leaves sailing down around her. Everything was molting, discarding color for the brown skin of autumn. Forgive me. Forgive me. She had suspected Eric wasn't being up front with her when he said it was over with Angela. But believing was easier, so she learned how. Things grew deceptively simple.

Inside the museum, she allowed her heart to slow down. The biking had been hard work, facing the wind. Her face felt flushed. She tied her sweatshirt sleeves around her neck and walked along, holding an empty sleeve in each hand. Sam was a visual artist. This was where she sorted things out, lost in the framed worlds on white walls. The bright lights and white tile floors rebounded energy back and forth; she stood right in the middle and soaked up the charge.

On her way home, Sam stopped at a paint store and bought a gallon of white paint, a roller, and a couple of brushes. The landlord said if she ever painted, she could deduct it from her rent. The living room had scotch tape marks and fingerprints everywhere. It was Saturday night, and the hours stretched out in front of her like an empty air strip.

Sam piled the room's sparse furnishings in the bedroom, collected all the artwork, and covered the floors with newspaper. She set the stereo in the kitchen and pushed up the volume. Reggae music filled the small apartment as lamps without shades cast curious shadows up and down each wall's face.

Drinking beer from the bottle, Sam moved with the music, bending her knees, keeping the white paint even, the strokes consistent. Sam first heard Bob Marley's music the year she studied at Bristol Academy in London. The white paint reminded her of the Easter holiday she spent in the Balearic Islands, one of Marley's old haunts. Whitewashed houses dotted the hillsides of Ibiza. She spent her time biking in the mountains, sketching the village plazas, dancing in discos at night.

Sam stepped back from the wall, remembering that long beach in the haze, the faceless man, and the sand. She felt the familiar pang of guilt. The same lines ran through her head. You drank too much. You should have known better. You should have known he was lying. You should have waited for your friends.

She had wandered out of the open air disco, looking for a friend who was studying with her at Bristol. The man grabbed her arm and headed towards the beach. "Where's my friend? I said I'd meet her here."

Sam remembered his choppy English. "You friend right down here. I bring you to her."

Before she realized it, Sam was lying on the sand, the man pulling at her clothes. Her head instantly cleared, conscious of what was happening. "I want to dance. Dance first."

She couldn't remember his face. Just hands pulling at buttons and zippers. "No. We do it now."

Sam ran her finger down his cheek. "Let's dance first. I want to dance. Then have lots of fun." She forced herself to kiss him, reaching her hand behind his neck.

Her stomach heaved. "You and me dance, yes?"

The man released a low, gurgling laugh. "Me and American woman dance. Okay. We dance."

SAM SWALLOWED the last of her warm beer and stepped back and looked at the white wall. "It never happened," she said. She had said the words before. "You used your head, and he didn't hurt you." But listening to her own voice, Sam remembered his dirty tongue pushing into her mouth, remembered the heaviness forced on top of her. The hurt was a deep mystery, a mixture of sadness and shame.

The three remaining walls looked dull gray in comparison. She put on a new album and started on the second wall. Leah would have to make up her own mind about dealing with Darin. Sam looked at the clock. It was eight-thirty. Leah would have called if things had gone badly. They were probably eating dinner out and making up right now. Fight, then make up. Fight again. Sam understood the pattern. She'd grown up in the middle of the ring.

She remembered the piece at the museum of the woman with four eyes. Each eye looked like it belonged; there was nothing unusual about the woman's face. Maybe she could see how things were; maybe two eyes were for looking back at the past and the other two were for everything else. Sam thought about that woman, eyes the green of peacock feathers looking out at her, looking back at an old lover, looking at poppies in a field, the reds so vivid you would swear they were beating hearts.

# 7

It was a slow day. Sam sat on the sidewalk, with her back against the doughnut shop, her sketch pad almost empty, and glanced down at the folded newspaper in her lap. She read the first few paragraphs of a story until she reached the fold of the paper, then began another. It was easier than drawing. The subjects weren't presenting themselves. The last bus rolled by the empty stop without slowing down.

The air was chilly. Sam reached into her backpack and pulled out the biking gloves she wore late in the fall. She could grip the pencil yet still retain a little warmth. Today would be the last good afternoon for drawing. It was getting too cold.

Sam folded a piece of drawing paper into an airplane. Rexel walked up, a smile spreading over his face. "You said you were an artist. First graders make those things," he said, kicking at the sidewalk with the toe of his shoe.

Sam didn't jump. "Well, Rexel Johnson. Nice to see you. Have yourself a chair." Sam motioned to her side, spreading out a part of the old army coat for him to sit on. He hesitated and then sat on the sidewalk next to the coat. "And who says adults can't make airplanes, anyway?" she asked.

"Nobody."

"Well, there you have it." Sam smiled and shrugged, taking aim for the trash can near the street.

Rexel looked at the open sketch pad next to her. "You ain't drawing."

"Listen to you! You ain't drawing. Is that what you learn in school? Jesus. I'm shocked." She looked straight in to Rexel's wide brown eyes. He looked away. "No one's been by worth drawing. It's what we in the business call a slow day. And I'm tired of drawing that trash can. Did that last week." Sam picked up the sketch pad again and pulled the pencil from behind her ear. "It's getting kind of cold, isn't it?"

"Yeah."

"I'm not that big a fan of winter. I like the sun."

"Oh, I bet it ain't that bad here."

"Aren't you from Minnesota?" Sam asked.

"Chicago. We moved here in May. It gets real cold in Chicago. The lake and the wind."

"Do you like it here or there better?"

"There." He paused and looked up the street. "I guess it don't matter either way."

"How about school?"

"School sucks, no matter where you are."

"You have friends here? Is the school as good? I guess they're teaching you to cuss. Or did you do that in Chicago?"

"You talk too much." Rexel's face was stone serious.

Sam laughed. "No one has ever told me that before. Not one living human being." She left a space between each word, overemphasizing. She caught the melting of lines on his forehead, sketched in the plane across his hairline. "I liked school. When we started finger painting in kindergarten, I figured it was going to be a place I'd like to hang out."

"You go to college?"

"Yep. Four years."

"Where?"

"Three at St. Cloud State. That's here in Minnesota. That's where I'm from, St. Cloud. And the fourth one was in England. London."

"How did you do that? You rich?"

"No. It was a scholarship. Boy, drawing the subways was the best. That's where I got interested in drawing people waiting around. Standing in line." She smiled. "Growing impatient."

"You like it there?"

"It was great."

"You go anywhere else?" Rexel pulled his hands from his pockets. The long fingers and large palms seemed a little out of proportion. Sam continued to draw, talking and looking up. "I traveled a little on holidays. I lived in a small stone cottage in Wales for the summer, drawing and biking around, then I ran out of money and had to come home. It's a nice place. Real quiet and full of smells,"

"Smells? Don't sound so great to me. Chicago smells."

"No. Unfamiliar smells, like coal burning in the fire-places and mixing with the thick morning fog. And green grass and daffodils in the spring. And the sea. Just a hint of the sea."

Rexel was quiet for a minute, visualizing it.

"You and your parents travel much?" Sam asked.

"Nope."

"Did your dad get transferred to Minneapolis or something?"

"Nope. I moved here with my mom." His jaw grew tighter, the tension showing in his hands as they curled into themselves again.

Sam paused, unsure if she should continue, yet knowing it would be more obvious if she didn't. "Did your dad die?"

"Not yet." Rexel turned his body to look down the avenue in the opposite direction.

Sam pulled a folder out of her backpack. "I brought something to show you if I ran into you. Want to see a sketch I did of my dog?"

Rexel turned around. His interest in the dog was apparent. Sam used it to draw him back out. He looked over at the picture. "That's pretty good. How did you make him sit still so long?"

"Oh, he doesn't have to sit still. I look at one feature at a time and sort of put it together piece by piece. Then, when he's sleeping or sitting quietly, I quickly sketch the whole thing. It kind of depends. Like you, for instance. I've done some preliminary sketches here." Sam pointed down to the paper with her pencil, shrugging her shoulders. "I'd like to draw you... if it's okay."

Rexel looked at the paper, at the frame of a face, the partial nose, the mouth. "You don't got any eyes." He directed his gaze off to the side.

"That's because you never let me see them." Sam motioned with her index finger and her shoulder for him to pull his head up, never touching him. She knew how important private space was, and this boy seemed to have a city block of it around him.

Rexel continued to look at the sidewalk. "If you let me draw you, I'll give you the finished product. I need the portrait for a class, but after it's done, it's all yours. A watercolor. It'll be dynamite. Probably make you rich someday." Rexel raised his head slightly, revealing deep cinnamon eyes.

"You are kind of strange," he said.

"Where do you and your mom live?"

"With my aunt on Blaisdell. It's a neat house. I have my own room in the attic. It's got all these corners everywhere and you can see the freeway from my window." Rexel looked right at Sam. "Some nights, I watch the lights and it's like I'm in a fort or something. It's pretty high up. When there's a wind or it's kind of foggy, like I'm on a big ship and I'm the last person alive."

He still stared at her. All those minutes with his eyes. His interest in the picture was obvious. Something inside of him made the sacrifice. All that time being vulnerable. Sam worked quickly.

"How come you girls put two holes in one ear and only one in the other?" Rexel asked, staring at Samantha's dangling earrings.

"That's art, Rexel," she said. "The unexpected balance of looking at the world with a perspective other than two by two."

"You're crazy."

"Fun though, huh? And incredibly interesting. Give me that. Contemplating getting an ear pierced?"

"Nope."

"Why? Don't you want to be a rock star when you grow up? What do you want to be?"

"Nothing. I'm never going to grow up. We'll never make it that long." Rexel was nonchalant.

"What makes you say that?"

"The bomb."

Sam stopped. "Wow. You really think about that? Man, when I was twelve, I was worried about what knee socks I had to match my shirt and if my bangs were ever going to grow out. If I'd ever get boobs. I guess things have changed."

Rexel shook his head. "When you were twelve, they probably stuffed people in phone booths and stuff like that too. I bet you didn't worry about nuclear bombs, if they were even invented yet."

"Give me a break. I'm not that old!"

"How old?"

"That old."

Rexel shrugged.

"Almost twenty-seven, and that's young for your information. I plan to live a long time. I worry about the nukes too, but it doesn't mean I don't take my dry cleaning out because I don't think it's worth it. I plan to get gray. I'm going to make a great old lady." Samantha looked down at the sketch pad, and then at Rexel. "If this turns out, I mean, if it's a masterpiece, I'll give it to you.

Okay? I appreciate your sitting for me. That's what we call it, a sitting."

"Well, I was sitting here to rest. If I'm going to model, where's the cash?"

"How about if I buy you a Coke? Inside?"

"I'll buy my own," he said, getting up and pushing his hands into his pockets.

"Jesus, you're stubborn." Sam gathered her things together.

"Beats crazy." Rexel walked into the doughnut shop ahead of her. At the table, Sam handed Rexel the sketch of Alexander. "Here, you can have this."

"No."

"Don't think it's good enough, huh?"

"It's good. But you don't got to give it to me."

"I know I don't have to, but I'm crazy, remember? I just want to."

Rexel looked down at the table, hiding his eyes, but not soon enough to conceal his pleasure. "Thanks."

"Anytime. And you should come and see him sometime. He's a neat dog. Lots of character. We could check it out with your mom."

"I make up my own mind," Rexel said. "I take care of myself. See ya." He shrugged his shoulders and backed away from the table.

For a moment, Sam wanted to stop him, to tell him all about how hard it was for her as a kid growing up on the

Mississippi River, how she was often afraid too, but she changed her mind. "Bye." She smiled and watched his back go out the door. It was going to be an excellent picture. Perhaps she'd do a series on kids. It was such a different chemistry.

## 8

"I want a simple black wood frame. Those metal ones look so tacky." The customer stood, her head tilted to the side as she studied the impression. "Isn't he darling? It's a second state. It's supposed to represent the sense of smell."

Sam looked at the Daumier lithograph of the little old man in the nightcap, smelling a potted plant on a crowded windowsill. She placed a frame corner on the piece. "How about this width?"

"Fine. Can I pick it up on Thursday? It's a gift for my father."

Sam nodded. "I'll try to get at it this afternoon or tomorrow. It'll be ready."

As the woman left, Bart walked in the front door, setting the bells jangling. "Morning, Samantha. What have we here?"

"Honore' Daumier. Political cartoonist and humanitarian." Sam pointed at the little round face. "Isn't he darling?"

Bart glanced at the piece as he walked by. "Nice. Want some coffee?"

"Thanks. I haven't had time to make any. Busy morning already."

"That's what I like to hear." Bart hung his coat on a hook behind the door and disappeared into the back room.

BART PLACED a cup in front of Sam. "Mary wants to get a swimming pool. Can you believe that? Fall in Minnesota and she talks about a swimming pool."

"Why now?"

"She says we have to plan ahead. We could only use the thing about two months out of the year. It's a crazy way to spend ten grand." Bart shook his head. "I haven't even got the damn deck paid for."

"You ought to be a Republican, Bart," Sam said. "You're starting to spend like one."

"It's not me, it's my wife! You should have a talk with her, convince her of the value of simplicity."

"We'll chat. I know, we'll do lunch and chat." Sam batted her eyes.

"Perfect," Bart said. "Problem solving the White House way."

Sam sat up on a high stool and began working on backing a print. "Hey, today's Halloween. Don't I get a bonus or something?"

"Right. You get a bonus, my wife gets a new swimming pool and just what do I get?"

"The bill?"

"I asked for that one."

"Yup."

SAM GOT off work at three o'clock and picked up some groceries at the co-op. Kids dressed in costumes were out trick or treating. She rode her ten speed to the doughnut shop, hoping Rexel might be around. She stopped and looked in the window. A pumpkin lay smashed on the sidewalk in front of her like a skull, split open and running out of itself.

"What's in the bag?" Rexel was standing behind her.

"You scared me!" Sam said.

"Good. It's Halloween." Rexel smiled. "So. Got any treats?"

Sam looked into the bag in her basket. "Yeah. Raisin bagels or whole wheat lasagna noodles. What's your pleasure?"

"I'll get doughnuts." Rexel dug into his jeans pocket.

"You mean you're buying for me too?"

"I guess. But only one. I only got seventy-five cents."

"Great. One sounds perfect." They walked inside and got a booth by the window. Sam pulled out a dollar bill. "How about getting a couple of milks on me?" Rexel took the money without hesitation.

"So, aren't you going out there? Are you too old to trick or treat?"

"That's for kids. Stupid day. Razor-blades and poison and x-raying candy and shit. Nobody should do it."

Sam nodded her head in agreement, her mouth full, powdered sugar on her lips.

"1 remember saving my candy and stashing it away," Rexel said. "One summer I found a melted clump of chocolate and paper in my baseball glove. The stain's still there."

"What are you doing today?" Sam asked.

"You mean here?"

"Yeah."

"Walking. I always walk after school."

"Thinking?"

"Yeah. I count my footsteps and I think about things." Rexel looked out at the street. Leaves caught in the wind and swirled against the curb. A bus coughed by, leaving a gray smoke hanging in the air.

"What are you thinking about now?"

"None of your business," Rexel said matter-of-factly.

"I better start home before it gets too dark," Sam said. "Thanks for the doughnut. Which way are you going?"

Rexel looked up at the clock. "Same way you are. I got some time to kill yet."

Sam walked next to her bike. "Doesn't your mom worry about you wandering around by yourself?" Sam asked after they'd walked awhile, both studying the sidewalk before them.

Rexel pulled a couple of leaves off a bush as they passed. "Some." He tore the yellowed foliage into small pieces, letting them sift through his fingers. "You do it, hanging out at bus stops, being so friendly, talking to everybody like some crazy bag lady." There was a pause. "I keep to myself. It's better."

"But I'm an adult," Sam said. "There's a difference."

"Some guy could put a knife to your throat. You ever wonder about that?"

"No. I don't live that way, Rexel. Worrying about what might happen. It isn't healthy."

"Then why are you quizzing me about walking around after school?"

Sam sighed. "Yeah. Okay. I get the point. I'll mind my own business." She stopped at the corner and turned to Rexel. "I'm going to ride now. I have to get home."

"Whatever." Rexel turned around, walking back the way he'd come.

Sam raised her voice. "See you. Thanks for the doughnut."

Rexel put his right hand up, fingers spread and waved once, not turning around.

## 9

Wrapped in a quilt, Sam sat at the kitchen table and wrote to her sister seven years her senior. The one she was convinced her parents wanted. The one who got away.

Dear Allison,

It's snowing. The wind is going crazy outside the windows, and I'm envisioning San Francisco. How are you? I don't suppose you're coming home for Thanksgiving? I wouldn't. But it would be nice to see you. What about Christmas?

How's Joe? I haven't seen Mom and Dad for a long time. I don't go home much, but I thought I'd make the obligatory Turkey Day showing. Things are much the same here. I'm not married. Not in love. Not seeing someone special. I've been dating a few guys. But, whatever. Maybe I need to get out of state. What do you recommend?

Mom sent me an article from the paper about Art Warden, that tall guy I went to prom with my junior year. Do you remember him? One date. Period. He owns some kind of store around there now. Refrigeration motors or something and he was in the paper as chairman of some charity fund drive this year. So why the article, you may ask. No letter. Just this snapshot of a balding guy I dated almost ten years ago. Jesus. They never change. If he sold furniture, he'd be perfect.

I could visit you one of these first holidays when I get together some cash. Avoid the entire scene at home. No toppled Christmas trees, no shouting matches, but it might not feel like Christmas without a few good tense words. I might skip going home this year. Make some excuse. Any excuse.

I'm still having those damn dreams, those nightmares. I just had one about the fourth of July. Everyone was fishing, lined up along the dock like little kids, dipping their lines into the water. Dad stood near the shore with a silver whistle in his mouth, his belly over the belt of his plaid Bermudas. He was starting some contest. Everybody ready, set, all that. Mom stood on shore, a huge purple bruise on her cheek. (Did he ever hit her much? What do you remember?) I was eight in this dream and wanted to catch the fish. I had to be the first one to pull one in. Remember the time he did that? A contest, I mean? You won. Remember? You got that sunfish. Well, in this dream, I got the first bite. The prize was a radio Dad got at the store for some promotion. I wanted that radio. I struggled to reel in the line, but it was so long. I kept watching Mom; she was looking into the water at her bruise, teetering over the water. I tried reaching for her, but my hands were glued to that damn reel. Pulling like crazy. Playing that fish.

Then the dream changed, and it was late at night, and I was the only one there, still reeling away and Mom's reflection was in the water, but she wasn't there. I was alone. God. What if I need a shrink? Do you think therapy would get me to blame you for catching the first fish? Hey, what if it's all our fault? Sibling rivalry or something? Ha ha.

Well. I don't enjoy spending my nights with nightmares. I'd much rather spend them with a man! Speaking of men, how is Joe? Are you ever going to subject him to a Minnesota visit? I'd like to meet him.

Did that friend of yours ever dry out? That old roommate? How did she do it? Did you talk to her? I'm still worried about Leah. I miss you. I hope you're happy. I do. Call me sometime.

Sam

## 10

_____

S now kept falling—over nine inches in the past twenty-four hours. Samantha invited Gary over for dinner. They had planned to go out to a movie, but many roads were impassible. Gary had a four-wheel drive; Sam's apartment was near a snow emergency route. He suggested stopping for some wine and a couple of steaks and fixing them at her house.

Sam spent the day cleaning and baking wheat bread. She sat down on the futon that served as a couch, looking around for stray laundry, old letters, private artifacts. She wasn't used to much company these days. The apartment was crowded with plants and pictures. Photographs clung to the woodwork frames of the doors: the cottage near Chepstow, her parents standing by the river at sunset, her first ballet recital pose. Sam was an artist; all her matted drawings rested on the floor along the wall. She smiled, shaking her head. "Alex, this place is looking like a personal shrine. Now, what are we going to do about that?" She bit her lip and pulled the dog onto her lap. The past clung to her like a child.

Midmorning, Sam bundled up and took the dog out for a little exercise. He floundered through the drifts in the yard. The snow was well past Sam's knees and near her waist in places. They stayed out about fifteen minutes. Despite the snow, it was cold; the windchill was thirty below.

Gary knocked at six-thirty, stomping his boots at the bottom of the stairs.

"Hey, Gar." Sam smiled. "How's the California boy doing tonight?"

"God, why did I move here, anyway?" Gary asked, pulling off his boots.

"Too much sun causes cancer. Remember?" Sam took the groceries as he reached the top of the stairs, giving him a kiss on the cheek. She put the bag on the table and linked her arm in Gary's.

"What a zoo. The roads they plowed are already filling back up. I bet we get a lot more by morning."

Alex was yapping at the intruder. Sam scooped the little dog up. "Come on in."

Gary smiled and rubbed his icy fingers together, looking at Sam. She wore a maroon wool sweater and jeans. Gray sweat socks. The apartment was toasty and had the aroma of freshly baked bread. He pulled off his stocking cap and shook the snow from it. "You have a dog?" He sounded surprised and irritated.

"No. This is my cat. The dog's in the other room." Sam shook her head, smiling. "Alex, meet Gary. Gary, Alexander."

"Charmed, I'm sure." Gary pulled off his down jacket.

"May I take your coat?"

Gary reached the parka toward her. "Thanks." Alex yipped one high-pitched bark. "Does he run on batteries?"

"He's protecting me. Don't worry, he'll calm down. Don't you like dogs?"

"Yeah. In cages, or on dog food commercials. They're okay on TV."

Sam rolled her eyes. "Well, he's welcome here." She put Alex on a pile of pillows in the corner of the living room and handed him a yellow tennis ball and an old high-top canvas shoe. The dog began gnawing on the sole of the shoe.

"Wine?" Sam walked into the kitchen, past Gary, who was still standing at the top of the stairs. She perched the corkscrew on top of the bottle, watching the abstract doll raise her arms as she pirouetted, the sharp point clutching the cork. "I've made a salad. You want to broil those steaks?"

"Sure." Gary turned on the oven and rolled up his sleeves.

"Some businesses may be closed on Monday," Gary said, breaking a long silence. "It doesn't look like it's going to let up." The steaks sizzled under the broiler flame.

"Wouldn't bother me. I could use the day off." Sam set the table and lit two slender candles. Alex came into the kitchen, interested in the smells of the cooking beef. Gary backed into him, causing a shrill yelp.

Sam picked up the dog, holding him under her left arm as she poured herself some more wine.

"So, how's your bus stop series coming?" Gary asked, holding out his glass. Sam drew people waiting around. Standing in line. Sometimes she worked in watercolor, but lately there was more charcoal. Rough, awkward lines. White space.

"Okay. I've been pretty busy."

"Have any shows planned?"

"Yeah, I'm trying to work up one for next fall."

"Really? Where?" Gary's voice marked disbelief.

"The institute might co-sponsor it. It's only in the planning stages, but we'll see."

"That's great."

Sam couldn't decide if his enthusiasm was genuine or feigned. She didn't trust compliments. She never had. He never seemed truly interested in what she did. It wasn't like her work was competition; he was a photographer. He had a show every year at the same gallery. But she was younger and a woman. Sam figured that probably mattered.

"Yeah," Sam said, rolling the stem of her glass between her forefinger and thumb. "I'm looking forward to it."

The table looked beautiful: a white linen cloth, golden wheat bread on a board, a salad filled with loud color, hand-dipped candles and steaks. Alex had eaten his dog food and sat at Sam's feet, whining. "No, Alex. Now bug off. You've had your share."

"Jesus. Can't you lock him in the bedroom or something?" Gary waved his glass at the dog. "Or better yet, the bathroom. We might use the bedroom later." He smiled, raising his eyebrows.

Sam's stomach tightened; her appetite disappeared. She looked at her half-eaten T-Bone. She picked up the brown and pink meat dripping with juices and dropped it in the dog's bowl. Alex tore at it, his tail wagging with excitement.

Gary followed her with his eyes as she crossed the room. She uncorked another bottle of wine. They had finished the first bottle rather quickly and both their reactions seemed slowed. She filled her glass and sat back down across the table from him.

"What was that about?" he asked.

"Can't we start this again?" Sam asked. "We're having a nice dinner. This is a date. Sort of. I mean, if you were allergic to him, I'd understand. If he bit you, I'd understand. But, well, if you just don't like him for no reason, well I guess," Sam paused, took a breath and exhaled. "It's too damn bad."

Gary dropped his fork on his plate. "Touchy." He stopped at that. No argument, no counterattack. He glanced into the dog's bowl. "It looks like we're done with dinner. Should we do the dishes now?"

Sam wanted to pull back. She didn't enjoy confrontation, and yet she had brought it on. "No need. I just throw them out the window when they get dirty." She smiled and put out her hand. "Friends?"

Gary took her hand, smiling, but shaking his head. "Friends."

"No need to even pick up the table. Alex will do that." She looked down at the dog, sitting next to her feet with the T-Bone stripped of meat between his front paws, chewing on the bone. "He is good for something."

Sam picked up her wineglass and headed into the living room and the stereo. She put on a reggae album and sat next to Gary on the futon. "This music always makes me warm." The last time, she'd said sure, why not. No good reason to say no. While they made love in his waterbed, she remembered summer school at college, lying on an air mattress in the quarries. Afternoons spent being a part of the turquoise water. A lily pad.

"You ever been swimming in a rock quarry?" she asked, leaning her head back against the wall. Gary put his arm around her.

"Yeah. They kind of give me the creeps, though. All that rock wrapped around you. Like a deep bowl. I'd rather swim in the ocean. Or a pool. Better yet, floating down a slow river on a raft."

"I liked being surrounded by all that rock. The cliffs hugging me. This quarry I swam in all the time in college was about forty feet deep. Crystal clear. You could see your feet when you tread water. Like white anemic fish swimming beneath you."

"I used to surf," Gary said. "Mostly, we partied on the beach. California. Sun, surf, and tons of people."

"I'd go out there and be all alone. It was pretty dumb, swimming alone. Cramps and all, but I liked it. Floating on that cold blue glass, feeling like I was being pushed on from the sky. Some hand applying just enough pressure."

"Speaking of oceans, I have another shoot on the east coast around the first of the year. You might like to fly out there with me, take a little time off from work, and spend a week in Boston. We could drive up the coast."

"That would be nice," Sam said after a while, her voice void of emotion. "God, I was glad to be getting away that August. Bound for Britain. I'd spend days out on the warm rocks, studying for my last summer classes, knowing I was leaving Minnesota and college and all of it. Finally getting out of the cramped apartments with parking lot parties. These no-mind football players used to bust their heads through the thin walls, drunk and numb, showing off."

Gary pulled Sam's hair away from her neck, letting it fall back, a small strand at a time. "What do you have against football players?"

"Only everything." Sam pictured Boston. She'd want to go to the aquarium and watch the fish. He'd want to go to some gym and get a workout. Or back to the hotel room. "I doubt I could get time off from work. I already took some vacation, and I want to save some for the summer. Anyway, I can't afford to take time off. And Bart needs the help."

"Yeah, I'm sure he doesn't mind having you around."

"What's that supposed to mean?" Sam asked. She had never said much about her boss.

"I've seen him. Beer belly, mid-forties. I'd bet ten to one he's lusting after you."

Sam leaned away from Gary, studying him. "Just because he's in his forties doesn't mean he's a jerk, Gary. Besides, you don't even know him. What makes you so protective?"

"I guess I'm jealous of other guys looking at you,"

Gary said, pouring more wine. "Even if he is married. I care about you."

Sam looked at the floor. Gary had never even been in her house before. He didn't know she had a dog. They had been out ten or fifteen times over the past year, and he was showing signs of territorial rights. The wine cast a curious haze on the conversation.

Sam held in an urge to giggle. "That's nice, Gary. I'm glad you like me. But I'm nobody's girl. I was a girl when I was twelve, but since then I've gotten my braces off, moved to the city and grown up. I don't see things that way. No license, no deed of purchase."

"Don't blow this all out of proportion, Sam. Christ, you're touchy tonight. I give you a compliment, say I care about you, and you've got me trying to purchase you at a slave auction."

"Ah, Gar. What are we doing, anyway? Aren't we just using each other for some company? We both like to go out and face it, we're just convenient. Let's not kid ourselves."

"What are you trying to say? Look, if you're not in the mood to jump in the sack, say so. Jesus, I figure there's over a foot of snow out there, so we're going to be here for a while. I just thought we could enjoy it." Gary got his jacket, which was thrown over the seat of her ten-speed bike, resting against the wall of the living room, and pulled out a pack of cigarettes.

"When did you pick up this quaint habit?"

"Get off my ass, Sam. Okay? It isn't funny anymore."

"Well, since we need to make the best of things, you'd better go outside and see if that Blazer of yours will start because there's no smoking in this apartment. That will give you time to inhale the thing. While the engine's warming up."

Gary dropped the cigarette on the wood floor and crushed it with his boot.

"You burn that floor and so help me."

"Enough, Sam. You want me to go, I'll go. I don't know what's gotten into you, but it was obviously not the right night for us to get together." He reached for his coat.

"Very perceptive, Gar." Sam reached over, broke a leaf off her jade plant, and began fingering it.

"Can I have a kiss goodnight before I go out in that shit?"

Sam wanted to slap his face. She wanted to head out to the rock quarries and dive deep, breaking the mirrored surface, but it was all too much work. She closed her eyes and kissed him on the lips for the last time. "If you have any trouble getting out, give me a holler," she said. Noticing the smile returning to his face, she added, "I'll come and help you push."

After he left, she picked up the kitchen. Everything seemed dirty. The dishes had a thick film of juice and solidified fat on them. The odor of cooked meat and smoke hung in the air. Two empty wine bottles stood on the counter. She lit the candles again to clear the air and started water for dishes.

The steaming hot water and dish soap mixed in with the smells of the kitchen. She wore rubber gloves and washed everything, scrubbing the counters and table, scouring the broiler pan. The music had finished long ago, but she didn't flip the album. It was the wrong time for Marley, the wrong time for music at all. Now she could clean and get things back in order. She put the dishes away, put the plant back on the center of the table and swept the floor. The work and the wine made her warm.

She pulled out a sketch pad, but threw it back on the floor before opening it up. Finally, she went to bed. Let the snow paint tonight. The transformations would be waiting for her in the morning. It was eleven o'clock. The phone rang.

"Sam?" It was Gary. "I just called to say I got home. The roads aren't that bad."

He had softened. He sounded apologetic. She hadn't been worried; she figured he'd get through, he'd make the vehicle do what he wanted it to. There had never been any question in her mind. She heard herself say, "I'm glad, Gary."

"I'm sorry about tonight. Maybe it's the weather."

"Yeah, maybe." Sam didn't sound convinced. "It's late, Gary. Good night."

"Good night. I'll call you," he added.

Outside, the snow fell in the streetlight's circle. Except for a couple of parked cars, it was impossible to tell the street from the neighborhood lawns. Huge drifts curved from house to house like waves, cresting and falling with the pull of a distant moon.

## 11

The Wednesday evening before Thanksgiving, Sam rode with Leah to St. Cloud. Darin was going skiing in Colorado. Leah was going home to be with her mother. She didn't believe people should spend Thanksgiving alone. Leah's parents split the same summer Sam threw the oboe in the Mississippi and moved in with Gran.

"I'm not sure if Allison told Mom and Dad that Joe was married. Anyway, I suppose I'll find out." Sam sat with her feet up on the dashboard of Leah's Celica. The lights from the dash highlighted everything a pale green.

"I thought he was divorced."

"In process, I guess. But they met when he was married. He's living with Allison."

"That must be weird. Knowing he has a wife."

Sam nodded. It wasn't surprising to her. Allison

seemed comfortable with it. Allison could take care of herself. She always had.

Her parents were watching television in the family room when Sam came in with her bags. They both looked up and smiled. "Well, hello Sam." Her mother. Warm. Stocking feet on the ottoman.

"Hi, Sam. How were the roads?" Dad. Coffee. A cigarette. The store's ad across his lap. Little red numbers scratched near the pictures of recliners. Lined up in columns. Totals.

"Okay. No snow yet." Sam sat down and pulled off her jacket and boots, fitting into the familiar portrait. "How's the store?"

Her mother rolled her eyes. "Dear, would you put those boots in the entry? You're melting on the carpet."

Sam took the boots out as her father yelled after her. "Got a sale on fabric recliners. Sales up on chairs eleven percent this month. You don't need a recliner, do you?"

"No. But thanks. I'm not the recliner type."

When Sam came back in, he was back to the calculator and her mother had hung up her jacket. Nothing had changed. They sat drinking coffee and watching Johnny Carson.

"You heard from Allison?" Sam asked.

"Christ." Her father, face behind the paper. "Were you aware she was sneaking around with a married man?" The paper was down now. That glare.

"Dad, what I knew doesn't matter at all."

"Like hell."

"It's her life. None of my business."

"I just don't understand how she could do it, that's all." Sam's mother shook her head. "We raised her better than that."

"Oh, come on, Mom. This isn't about potty training and manners. She loves him."

"That's what you think raising a child is? Teaching her to control her bowels? Well, I like to believe we had more influence than that. Morals. Values."

"Sure. Whatever." Sam gave in. It didn't matter. This was just the way it was.

Her father looked up again. "Don't patronize us, Samantha."

"I'm not."

"Well, yes, you are." Her mother this time.

"Sorry. I'm sorry. I'm sorry for me. I'm sorry for Allison. Hell, I'm even sorry for Joe…"

"Don't cuss in this— "

"I'm sorry for cussing. I'm sorry for whatever you like. Now, can we drop this?"

The three of them turned to the TV and buried the discussion as they often did. The rest of the evening, they talked and said little, and then they went to bed.

Sam woke to the aroma of turkey roasting and coffee and cinnamon. Her mother was a wonderful cook. There would be cinnamon rolls and fresh fruit set out on the table. It was comforting. Waking up to the pleasant past, the times when everyone laughed and lived together like a family. The days without sparks. And there were such days. It was because of them she moved home the summer after seventh grade. She missed her parents. The house. The river. Her own room.

Mr. and Mrs. Ellings had gone to counseling. They were getting it together. At least they were trying. I must have meant something to them, Sam told herself. They were working at it.

THANKSGIVING DINNER. A beautiful dining room filled with glorious food. Candles. Flowers. A table full of guests. Elmer sat next to Sam. He had worked at the furniture store for twenty-three years. Sam grew up calling him Uncle. "Say, Sami. Do you got any fella down in the city ready to ask you to marry him?" Elmer wore a brown plaid shirt and a navy tie. He wore the same tie every year and asked the same questions. Sam smiled and raised her eyebrows. "Two or three, Uncle, two or three."

An old neighbor said Sam was looking rather thin and kept sending food around her way. Sam looked at her watch. Her father sat at the head of the table. "Say, Sam, do you have any need for a nice coffee table? You don't have one, do you? I got a display model with a minor scratch on the top. Nothing much. Nice little maple piece."

Mrs. Ellings stepped behind him with a fresh bowl of mashed potatoes. "Dear, Sam doesn't want a lot of stuff. She said she'd let us know if she needed anything, didn't you, honey?"

Sam felt like she was six again, being talked about at the table. Everyone told her what she felt, why she acted the way she did. "I don't need anything, but thanks." Out of the corner of her eye, she could see her father shaking his head. "Isn't the next question from someone here going to be, have I gotten a different job? Do I still do that art stuff? Why did I ever move to Minneapolis, anyway?" She sighed. It was so predictable.

Mrs. Ellings stood up. "I'll get the pies. Anyone ready for dessert?"


AFTER DINNER AND DISHES, Sam spent some time in the back sunroom sketching the river. Immense windows opened up onto the backyard and the shore. A willow, an oak, and several pines framed the small swimming beach. They didn't have much snow here yet, drifts sprawled across the yard between patches of dead grass. Leaves stuck in the fence around the flower gardens. Everything was brown. Wrinkled and dead. Years ago, they built bonfires on the beach with the leaves. Sam burned marsh-mallows and watched the stars come on. Allison told ghost stories and brought boys around, telling Sam to go into the house or she'd send a ghost after her. Sam was still in grade school and believed Allison could do it. Many nights she spent sneaking around to see her sister kiss a boy, not wanting to miss anything.

It was always difficult to be home; the ghosts were everywhere. Some remained from bonfires and pleasant campouts in the backyard when Sam and Allison watched the moon light up the sky through the princess willow tree. Dad ran out with a canning jar to help catch fireflies. There were stories and fairy tales. Some ghosts sat on the back balcony baying at the moon like lonely timber wolves. Howls so painful they could crack the night sky in two.

## 12

"Didn't I say to dress warm, Rexel Johnson? Where's your hat?" Sam stood at the bus stop when Rexel walked up. They had run into each other again, in the middle of the week, and decided to take a field trip out to the New Minnesota Zoo. It was Saturday morning, and it was cold.

Rexel turned around, half smiling, and rolled his eyes. "You aren't for crap at saying hello."

Sam rubbed her mittens together. "I'll work on it. Hello. How are you?"

"Where did you get the weird socks?"

"They're leg warmers. Remember, I said to dress warm? Flashy, huh? Bright lime like caterpillars and luna moths. They're art all by themselves, Rexel."

"So you been to this zoo before?" Sam nodded. "Why are you going again?"

"God, you ask a lot of questions, Rexel. I like to look at the animals, and walk around in the cold and wear fluorescent leg warmers and a big puffy coat and embarrass you, okay?"

"Okay."

Once on the bus, Sam sat and looked around her. There weren't many people riding. Rexel sat looking out the window, his hands resting on his lap, relaxed and open. "Last time. Who did you go to the zoo with?" he asked, still looking out the window.

"A guy named Gary. He's a friend."

"You his girlfriend?"

"Nope."

Sam thought about Gary. It was last winter. They'd bundled up in long johns and jeans. Two pairs of everything. He was all right, a pretty nice guy. She couldn't put her finger on the problem.

"You got a boyfriend?"

"Nah." Sam pulled the white stocking cap lower on her head, forming a huge collar of thick hair beneath it. "Men are a lot of work."

"Everybody's a lot of work," Rexel said. "They got lions at this zoo?"

"Yeah. I'm not sure what will be outside in the big pens, but we might get lucky."

Stepping off the bus, Sam shuddered in the stiff wind.

"I can't believe you didn't bring a hat. You're going to freeze your ears."

"You're worse than my ma. She doesn't even bitch about that."

They crossed the parking lot. Sam raised her voice, teasing. "Okay, fine. Get defensive. Use foul language. You're going to be cold. That's just facts." They walked inside and paid. "I'd like to get some gum. There's a gift shop. Want to go in with me?" Sam smiled. "Still friends?"

Rexel rolled his eyes. "Yeah, I guess. Don't ask me why, though."

He walked ahead of her, pushing open the door, letting it go.

"Great," Sam said out loud. "This is a great kid."

Sam found Rexel looking at postcards. He glanced over at the stack of T-shirts and some stocking caps with the zoo insignia of a moose on them. He walked up and grabbed a hat. "I might get one of these. They're only four dollars."

"A deal, no doubt." Sam smiled.


OUTSIDE, several bison stood in a group near the high chain-link fence. Their long shaggy coats resembled huge old dust mops, multi-shaded tufts of fur hanging close to the ground. Sam turned to Rexel. "I want to get a picture. Will you stand there a minute?"

"You want a picture of the buffalo?"

"Yes. The buffalo and yes, you. Okay? You let me draw you, didn't you?"

"All right. But then I get to take one." Rexel looked at the thirty-five-millimeter camera. "Nice."

Sam smiled and squinted into the bright light. "Thanks." This was such a new role for her. She might want a child of her own someday, might want to be a mother. Kids were so easy to be with. Not demanding too much. Rexel stood with his hands in his pockets in front of the fence. She took a couple of shots.

"You said one picture."

"The odds are that one of those will be good. Have to cover for human error. Your turn." Sam pointed out the buttons and walked over to the fence.

"Ready?" Rexel closed his right eye. His lip pulled up into a crooked smile.

Sam flexed her biceps and smiled. "Go for it!"

After he took the picture, Rexel focused on the buffalo. "Look at the bull all by himself." Sam said. "Big, isn't he?" Steam rose from the animal's deep black nostrils. Rexel took another picture. "I'll get copies for you," Sam said. Rexel paused and looked at her, then advanced the film and took several more.

"Aren't they beautiful, though?" Sam asked. "I always feel bad when I see them penned up."

"Why'd you come then? That's what zoos are."

Rexel's immediate irritation surprised her. "I guess it's better than little square cages and never being outside."

"They got it as good as anybody else." Rexel's voice was sharp. "Everybody has to worry about being extinct. It don't matter. We're all going to die before it gets figured out, before anybody does anything." He looked at the ground and held Sam's camera out to her. His arm was shaking.

Sam took the camera with one hand and reached for Rexel's wrist with the other. His hand formed a fist, filled with tension. "I know you feel that way, Rexel, but it doesn't have to be like that. I figure if we're intelligent enough to visit other planets, we can figure out how to keep from blowing ourselves up."

"Yeah, well, we aren't doing so hot now."

"Well, not yet, but we can. You shouldn't let it wreck your life. I mean, you can't go on a picnic always worrying about rain. You wouldn't have any fun."

Rexel looked straight at her, his chin tucked close to his chest. "But, shit, it rains all the time, Sam. It just keeps on raining."

"It's not raining now, Rexel." Sam looked at Rexel. "It's a beautiful day, and you and I are friends."

Rexel looked up at the empty sky. "Yeah, well, your ma ain't real sick either. You just don't know that much about it." His voice didn't sound angry, just tired. Sam was taken by surprise. She didn't want to ask; not knowing was easier.

"I'm thirsty. I have a thermos of hot chocolate in my backpack. Want some?"

Rexel nodded, blinking back the tears. They stood, not talking, sipping the hot milk. Steam and pleasant smells climbed out of the cups into the open air. Snow crunched as the buffalo walked along, nosing the ground for hay, staring at the two as they stood nearby.

Rexel made a fist. "You ever feel the blood pumping inside you, in your veins?"

"Sometimes." Sam said. She felt tired.

Rexel sighed. "Sometimes I think about what's inside me, like there could be an entire city in there, another complete universe, millions of times smaller than this one. And it might have rush hour sidewalks all crowded and fires and riots and stuff. And too many cars for the streets to handle. Like things had to bump around to get by." Rexel picked up a chunk of snow and started shoving it through the fence. "And when my stomach rumbles, it might be a tiny earthquake, and things are splitting open, wrecking homes and flower gardens. Everything turned upside down."

Sam stared into the distance, squinting. "I used to

imagine when I ate Cheerios, they were all soldiers floating in the ocean on little life preservers. Their ship sank, and if I saved them with my spoon, they wouldn't drown. It made eating the soggy ones at the end easier, I suppose."

Rexel smiled, then exhaled as if blowing a smoke ring.

"I'm cold. Want to go inside and check out the whale tank?" Sam asked.

"If I can walk. Maybe my toes are frozen."

"Maybe, but maybe not."

REXEL'S MOUTH hung open as soon as they entered the marine exhibit. The tension sifted out of his shoulders. He walked along, keeping his hands on each new aquarium tank, his nose close to the glass, dragging his feet.

They had the exhibit almost to themselves. Sam carried on conversations with the fish, talking most of the time, narrating the displays as if it were their own underwater home and Rexel was meeting the neighbors. A man with a pale complexion stood at the end of the exhibit, staring at Sam. She kept talking. "I wanted a dolphin for my bathtub when I was a little girl. I watched every 'Flipper' episode. Mom and Dad weren't any more interested in getting a dolphin than they were in getting a seal. I got that idea from a Disney movie. We lived on a river; I couldn't see the problem."

Rexel watched the dolphins curl past, his eyes wide. As he followed one down to the corner of the glass viewing area, a beluga whale swam up, looking at the observers. Rexel jumped back. He held his hand out, open-palmed against the glass as the whale came around again. The graceful creature captured the water and made it move as if commanded, its vast body curving and gliding through the tank. "He wants to be friends, Rexel!" Sam stepped back and focused her camera. The frame included Rexel's back, his hand outstretched on the glass, the fingers reaching in every direction. Long, slim hands. Deep brown with shadows of cream between the fingers. When the whale swam around again, Sam pushed down the shutter. Rexel didn't even seem aware of her. She walked around to the side and got his profile. Such a face.

"What are you thinking about?" Sam had finished the film and stood next to Rexel for several minutes.

"I'd like to be somebody that studies these when I grow up, if I grow up," he added without a pause.

It was the first time he'd even acknowledged such a possibility to her. "A marine biologist, perhaps?" Rexel nodded. "Then you could live in some exotic ocean paradise and I could visit you. I thoroughly approve."

They reached the end of the exhibit, and Sam noticed

the man in gaudy plaid pants was still standing there. He smiled at her. "Hi." He sounded like a child.

Sam smiled back. "Hello. How are you?" Rexel shot Sam a quick scowl. The man shifted his feet. He wore a sweater with a shirt underneath, the tails sticking out.

"Who's that?" He pointed at Rexel.

"This is my friend." Sam pushed Rexel along ahead of her. "Goodbye."

"Who's that?" The man repeated himself, louder this time.

Sam turned the corner outside and glanced at Rexel; he shook his head again. "Why'd you talk to him?"

"Because he talked to me," Sam said.

"He was weird." Rexel pushed his hands into his coat pockets.

"Oh, I'm sure he was harmless. He just wanted to talk."

Rexel faced Sam. "How come you always smile? Like everything is fun and nobody is going to hurt you? Sometimes you are kind of dumb, Sam." He shook his head.

"Look, Rexel, that's how I deal with things. I like to smile at people, and I can take care of myself too. I know you talk like having lived in Chicago gives you a corner on that market, but it's not true. Some hard things have happened in my life too, and I decided smiling helped, okay? So just cut me some slack, huh?" She walked through the door and let it go.

Rexel walked down to another exit.

They met up in the hallway. Rexel's hands were deep in his pockets. "Sometimes, I get scared. Just scared that everybody is going to get on a bus and ride away."

"Do you want to talk about your mother, Rexel?"

"Yeah, maybe sometime," he whispered. They walked along together, not saying anything. They walked into the tropical garden house. Lush green plants. Steamy moist air. Monkeys swung from their tails, chattering together. A huge colorful bird screamed high over their heads.

## 13

It was Saturday morning; Sam faced another depressing weekend without plans. Standing at the window of her apartment, surveying the neighborhood after the latest snowfall, she looked up a telephone number and dialed the phone. The pines in the front yard drooped with the weight of the fresh snow, bending down, touching the drifts beneath the branches. There was no answer, so she dressed warmly and walked down to the doughnut shop. She saw Rexel at the park, throwing snowballs at the basketball backboard.

"Rexel!" She made a snowball and missed the board entirely.

"Larry Bird you ain't."

"What's up?"

"Nothing. What are you doing over here?"

"I'm having a Christmas party tonight. Well, I just decided to. Want to come?"

"What?"

"A party. At my house. Ask your mom if it's okay. She can come too if she wants. It's just going to be my friend Leah and I. I thought it would be fun. Oh, it was a dumb idea."

"Yeah, pretty dumb. Why you want a kid at your party? And I don't know your friends."

"Friend. Just one. And I don't care if you're a kid. We're just going to eat and play cards or something. Probably a dumb idea. Never mind."

"I'll come over,"

"Would your mom let you? How's she doing, anyway?"

"She isn't home. I make up my own mind."

"How about your aunt?"

"I'll give her your address. It's cool."

"Okay then." Sam nodded. "It could be fun. I'll see you about six-thirty. Don't eat, okay?"

"Yeah. I might see you then." Rexel threw another snowball and made it through the bare hoop. "Two points." He smiled.

Sam walked home and called Leah. It would be nice to have Rexel meet someone new. Leah was a lot of fun. "And Leah, I've invited my little friend, Rexel. Now you'll get to meet him. He's kind of shy. I'm telling you that right away, so don't scare him, okay?"

Leah laughed. "Right, Sam. I'll keep it low key. So what are we going to do, play games?"

"Six o'clock, Leah. See you then." Leah would be there at five-thirty. She was an obsessive early arriver. Sam had to get groceries and bake some cookies.

Sam had made all the Christmas tree decorations over the years. She even had a popsicle-stick sleigh she made in the third grade. Her mother saved it for her and gave it back to her last Christmas. She plugged in the lights at about three o'clock and sat on the futon with a cup of coffee, waiting for the cookies to get done. She hoped Rexel liked tacos. Anything Mexican would be fine with Leah. In college, after they'd been out drinking, they'd always hit the taco stand for a couple of tacos or burritos.

The lights pushed a warm glow onto the white walls, splashing across the prints and sketches scattered on the carpet. Sam's last charcoal portrait of her grandmother rested along the wall near the tree. "Merry Christmas, Gran," she said out loud. "I'll talk Bart into a free frame from the shop. It's about time you got up on the wall."

Sam hugged herself and smiled, looking at the colorful lights. She looked at the Picasso poster from the Walker Art Center exhibition. A London subway map hung above a pile of overstuffed pillows in the corner. A huge dieffenbachia stretched in front of the windows, reaching shadows out into the room. The light was already fading in the mid-afternoon. It felt good to see her belongings, to ruminate over the conditions when she attained them, to keep the past and the present blended. Sam enjoyed living alone, enjoyed having her whims, her attachments front and center.

Sam listened to reggae on the stereo while she chopped the tomatoes, green onions, and olives for tacos. She slipped a chunk of tomato to the dog. Sam sang along with Bob Marley's familiar lyrics as she filled small bowls with chunks of color.

When Leah arrived at five-thirty, Sam was wrapping a couple of presents. Several packages were already under the tree.

"Merry Christmas," Leah walked in carrying a huge, loosely wrapped gift. She walked over and leaned the present against the wall near the tree.

"What in the world is that?" Sam poked the paper, looking for a loose place to peek.

"You'll find out soon enough. Now get away from there." Leah was petite and blonde. She had manicured nails and was dressed fashionably. Designer tastes. "Aren't you going to offer me a drink? Or is this party dry because the kid is coming?"

"I'll get you some wine, big mouth." Sam put her hands into the huge pockets of her denim skirt. "Red or white?"

"Both. A glass for each hand."

"Been a tough week, huh?"

"Ah, you could say that. Darin's been working late hours for about a month now. Says he has this enormous project. I hardly ever see him. Anyway, how are you?"

Sam walked toward the kitchen. "Fine. There's always a lot to do at Christmas. I'm doing a piece for my parents. I've never given them any of my work before, not that they'll like it or anything, but it's all that I can afford. It's a picture of the river, that big oak and the bench they always sit on to watch the sunset. It'll be okay, but it's taking forever. "

"Oh, they'll like it." Leah twisted her earring with her left hand. "Heard from Gary since your little date during the storm?"

"Yeah. He's called a couple times. I've always said I'm busy, but I should just come out and tell him to get lost." Sam disappeared into the kitchen.

Leah raised her voice. "Oh, that would be subtle. Very sensitive. You're starting to open up with men, Sam. I'm so glad you've been on the level with him."

"Leah, no lectures." Sam came back with a glass of wine in each hand. "1 decided on red. Fits the season."

"Well, too bad about Gary. He was a good-looking guy."

"Big deal, Leah. You're so shallow." Sam rolled her eyes. "And what's this past tense? He still is good looking." She sat down on the floor, crossing her legs under the tent of her skirt. She wore fuchsia anklets without shoes. "Look. He drove me nuts. He was a nice guy most of the time, and then he'd look at me like that, you know, that macho-horny-touchy look and I'd want to throw up. I'm not anybody's property."

"Don't you ever want to get married and raise a family?"

"That sounds like a John Denver song, Lee. And you should talk. When are you going to do it?"

"I want to. We might get married this spring. I've brought it up, but Darin hasn't said much. I think I'd like to have kids and if we're going to, we may as well get started."

"You think you might like to have kids? Said with conviction. Hey, meeting Rexel might be a good test to see how you like being around bigger kids, because they grow up into teenagers, you know." Sam took a sip. "Rexel's a good kid."

"Since when were you such a kid lover, anyway?" Leah asked. "You thinking about trying the parenting idea too?"

"Nah. I just got interested in kids when this lanky boy with a big attitude started giving me a hard time for sitting on the sidewalk and being strange. He is funny and has these greatest eyes, like they're always some place far away, thinking about god knows what. He thinks the world's a hell of a place, like being born was somebody's idea of a joke and any minute we're all going to pay and get blown off the earth."

"Sounds like a fun kid," Leah said.

"He is. You'll like him."

Sam ran down to answer the door. Rexel stood at the step, holding a tin in one hand, shifting his weight from one leg to the other.

"Come on in, Rexel, I have a friend I'd like you to meet." Rexel pushed his free hand deep into his pocket, looking at Sam with panic in eyes. At the top of the stairs, Alexander barked in high-pitched gulps. "This is Alexander, Rexel. My dog and loudmouth guard. He's all bark; he won't bite."

Rexel handed the cookie tin to Sam and kneeled down by the dog, petting him. Alex stopped barking and wagged his tail, leaning into Rexel's hand. "Rexel, this is Leah Thomas. Leah, Rexel Johnson. Leah and I grew up together in St. Cloud. We went to high school and college together. Leah lives in Minneapolis too."

"Hi." Rexel's voice was tentative and soft.

"Nice to meet you, Rexel. I've heard a lot about you."

There was an awkward silence. Rexel walked over to the window, looking into the yard, both hands cemented in his jeans pockets. Sam pulled her hair up into a tail and glanced at Leah, shrugging her shoulders.

"Rexel, would you like a can of pop? I've got Coke, Dr. Pepper and Seven Up. Oh, and Gatorade."

"I'll try that, thanks. Never had Gatorade before." He sat down on the floor next to Alex and began petting him, absorbed in the dog.

"What's in the tin?" Sam asked when she handed him his drink.

Rexel shook his head in embarrassment. "A fruit cake thing. My aunt got it at work or something. It might not be any...."

"Well, how nice," Sam interrupted. "Thanks. I have a little something for you too, but it'll have to wait until after we eat."

Rexel's shoulders relaxed. "You like Mexican food?" Sam asked as she walked toward the kitchen again. Rexel didn't answer. She turned around, spinning on her tiptoes, her full skirt twirled in the air. "Tacos? Burritos?"

Rexel nodded. "Yeah." He looked down at the floor.

"I've drafted Leah to help me in the kitchen; you can play catch with Alex." Rexel's eyes pulled up. "There's a green ball in that basket by the stereo. He's a rotten catcher, but he tries hard."

Rexel got up and headed for the basket. Sam nodded at Leah, motioning toward the kitchen. "You can put on some music if you'd like. The power switch is on the side." Leah followed her into the kitchen.

Rexel sat on the floor by the stack of records. Alex

curled up in his lap. "Quiet kid," Leah mouthed, once in the kitchen.

"Usually not this quiet," Sam whispered. "He'll get over it." She got out the hamburger. "You want to brown this Lee while I cut up some lettuce?"

"If I'm forced."

"I'll fill your wine glass."

"Deal."

Old Crosby Stills Nash and Young music filtered out of the living room. Sam shouted, "You like this stuff? I thought you were too young to have heard of them."

Rexel didn't answer. Sam walked over to the archway and looked into the living room. Rexel was holding the ball up and Alex stood quivering in anticipation. "A good choice." She smiled.

"My cousin in Chicago had this record. He was old too. Course not as old as you." Rexel smiled. "You got any more Gatorade? It's pretty good."

The three of them sat around on the living room floor eating tacos and burritos. Sam suggested the floor over the kitchen table. She said it was more comfortable and more festive, with the tree lights covering the room with color. Alex sat near Rexel, watching every move from his hand to his mouth. Rexel looked over at Sam. "He eats olives?"

"Alex eats most anything. But if you feed him, he'll bug you all night."

Rexel held a small ring of black olive out for the dog. Alex snapped it out of his fingers. Rexel smiled and started eating again. The dog sat up on its hindquarters, whining and turning his head from side to side.

"See, I told you. Now he won't stop until he's had his fill of your taco. You may as well surrender your plate. I do not know where that dog got his manners."

"The first time I fed Alex," Leah said. "I gave him a couple of crumbs from this piece of cheesecake. I'd stopped at a bakery and gotten two pieces of this great stuff, and Sam and I were going to pig out. Well, I fed him this crumb and went to get a glass of milk. When I came back to the table, he was standing on it, next to my empty plate, licking his chops. I don't swear much, but that dog got an earful. I haven't fed him since."

"Yeah," Sam added, "and she tried to talk me into giving her my piece because my dog had taken hers. Of course, it was too late. I eat almost as fast as Alex does."

"Didn't you see him on the table?" Rexel asked.

"Nope. I was eating at the counter with my back to him. He's quick. If I'm cooking I have to be careful not to leave it unattended. He jumps from the chair to the counter. I've tried to break him of the habit, but I guess he likes food as much as I do."

After clearing away the dishes, Sam said, "Time for Santa's presents." She handed a brightly wrapped present to Leah and one to Rexel. "Merry Christmas, you two."

Leah pulled the huge present out from along the side of the tree. "All right, Sam, guess what it is."

"An ironing board?"

"Nope."

"A skateboard?"

"Jesus."

"A board of directors? A mirror?"

"Okay, forget the guessing. We'd be here until Easter."

Sam glanced at Rexel and saw his active fingers memorizing the seam of his jeans. She reached for the tin with the ribbon on top. "And this is from Rexel." She opened the tin, feigning surprise. "A fruit cake! How nice."

"But I didn't get you anything."

"This is something, Rexel, thanks. You know how I like food. We'll eat some later. Now open yours. Go on."

"You weren't supposed to do this," he said. "I didn't know..."

"Jesus, Rexel. Open it up. Come on."

He tore at the paper, pulling out a T-shirt that had "hello minnesota" printed on it. "That's for surviving your first Minnesota winter. Technically, it's not over yet, but by the time you can wear the shirt, it will be."

"Thanks." Rexel shrugged, smiling. "It's nice."

"Don't mention it. Now, Leah, your turn."

Leah was sitting back, staring off into the other room. She blinked. "What?"

"Open your present," Sam said.

"Nope. You haven't opened mine yet."

Sam tore the paper off the huge present. It was a reclining lawn chair. "Thank you! I can sit in the back-yard and get some sun."

"Not today," Rexel said, looking out the window at the sparsely falling snow.

"Well, when you can wear your T-shirt, I'll be trying out my chair. Until then I can sure use it in here. This will be the first real chair in the living room. Both times my parents have stopped by, they have had a fit that I don't have furniture. Just those silly mattresses on the floor. Since they own a furniture store, they think I want a load of stuff that I'd have to haul around every time I move. But this… now this is compact and convenient. Thanks, Leah."

Leah was already opening her gift. It was a pair of leopard print slipper socks with suede soles. "I can use these right now. Very punk, Sam. I love them."

Rexel looked confused. Sam laughed. "You don't like my taste in clothes, do you, Rexel?"

"You picked out a nice T-shirt," he said. "I guess there's hope."

Rexel left to catch a bus at eight-thirty. He got his coat and the T-shirt and wrapping paper, taking all of it with him. "Thanks, Sam." He looked up at her, straight into her eyes. It was so much easier to understand him now, to know what he wasn't saying. He looked over at Leah. "Nice meeting you."

"Thanks for the fruitcake. That was very thoughtful. Tell Mrs. Johnson Happy Holidays for me." Sam put her hand on Rexel's shoulder. "Have a wonderful Christmas, Rexel. And enjoy your vacation."

"Yeah. You too."

"I'll call you next year, huh? We can go ice skating or something."

Rexel laughed, a relaxed low rumble. "Yeah, I guess. I can't wait to see what you'd wear out on the ice."

Sam rolled her eyes and pushed him toward the door. She watched him cross the street and walk to the bus stop from her living room window. It was dark and she couldn't tell if he was looking, but she waved and then stood there until the bus pulled up.

Leah was pouring herself another glass of wine. "This one's shot," Leah slurred. Sam took the bottle and walked into the kitchen. She put on some water for tea. "Okay, Sam," Leah said. "I give. What's the joke?"

Sam walked back into the room and sat down on her lawn chair. "What do you mean?"

"The kid's Black. You never told me he was Black. I mean, you've been talking your head off about this kid and never said he was Black! What's the attraction here, anyway?"

Sam put the chair in the upright position. "I thought I told you. If I never mentioned he was Black, I'm sorry. I never said he had curly hair either, but that doesn't seem to bother you. What difference does it make, anyway?"

Leah puffed out her cheeks, releasing the air. "Don't get so huffy. I just don't get it. I mean, I felt like we were babysitting tonight. Why are you hanging around this kid?" She turned to Sam.

"I like him. He's a nice kid. He's interesting and witty and..."

"And twelve years old? I think you need your head examined. Are you attracted to him?"

"Leah, you've had too much to drink. Again. And I don't appreciate these insinuations about me being some kind of sexual pervert just because I think kids are just as interesting to be around as adults. In fact, sometimes more interesting. You've mentioned this before, and it pisses me off. I thought you'd understand when you met him. I thought you'd like him too." Sam stomped out of the room and slammed the bathroom door.

When she came back out, Leah was making the tea. "Herbal or otherwise?" Leah asked, one hand on her hip.

They both laughed. "Herbal. Cinnamon Rose, please." She paused as Leah tore open the cellophane on the box of tea, exaggerating her gestures. "Bitch." Sam said.

Leah turned and stuck out her tongue. "Bitch." She poured water over the bags in the cups. "Look, Rexel's a nice enough kid. Don't get me wrong. It's just that I've known you all my life and I've never envisioned you as the motherly type. And I don't understand what you and a Black boy have in common."

"I don't want to be his mother. I just want to be his friend." Sam dunked the tea bag, letting it twirl in the air between dunks. "There aren't that many people I like to be around these days. Everybody seems to have some kind of agenda. I invited my friends to this party, and they both showed up. Perhaps there is something wrong with me, but I had a good time. A damn good time." Sam walked out with her cup. "I'm going into the living room and watching the lights. They're putting on a show. Join me if you want to."

## 14

S am arrived at the party comfortably late. She knew there would be a crowd, and people were easier to meet after they'd had a couple of drinks. She wore long, dangling rhinestone earrings and lipstick.

Leah answered the door in a glittery silver tunic and tight stretch pants. She smiled, holding a cigarette in her right hand. "Enter, dear friend."

"Since when did you take up that disgusting habit?" Sam asked, her hands on her hips.

"Happy New Year to you too, buddy." Leah had been drinking for a while. She shuddered and blew smoke over her right shoulder. "Everyone seems to be giving it up for a New Year's resolution, so I decided I'd start."

"Give it to me, Leah Thomas." Sam took the cigarette and brushed past Leah, putting it out in the nearest ashtray. "Now, why don't you be a good hostess and show your best friend where she can put her coat and get a drink."

The condo was immaculate. People stood around like animated models, holding drinks and talking, occasionally waving a free hand. Leah and Darin moved into the condo in December. They were renting with an option to buy. Sam played with the garbage disposal and the ice machine in the refrigerator's door every time she came over. Everything was white; the walls, the fixtures, the lamps. Leah had taken her Dayton's charge card and bought the living room and bedroom. Everything looked as if she had positioned it for a perfect composition.

The two women worked their way back to the bedroom. Leah threw Sam's coat on the bed. "Great dress. I haven't seen that, have I?" Leah asked.

"Nope. It's a vintage number from Ragstock. I bought it with Christmas money from my sister. You like it, huh?" The dress was black velvet with a deep cut back. Rhinestones circled the neckline, drizzling down the front of the dress.

"It's very nice. You look so damn skinny I could kill you."

"Save it, Leah. You look gorgeous."

Leah shrugged, brushing fine blonde hair off her shoulders. "Let's go get a drink. I'm thirsty."

Sam caught Leah's arm. "Is everything okay? You seem a little edgy."

"I'm fine, Sam. Darin and I had a few words before the party, that's all. Over some goddamn gin. I bought the wrong stuff or something. But it's nothing. I just don't bounce back from an argument as fast as he does. He's already been on the make with about three women tonight and it's only ten o'clock."

Sam looked at the floor. "That bastard."

Leah's eyes opened wide. "It's not that bad." She bit a fingernail.

Sam put her arm around Leah's shoulder and gave her a hug. "Okay, then. Let's go get some goddamn gin, or how about some goddamn scotch? You got any scotch?" Sam laughed as they walked into the kitchen.

Many of the faces were familiar. Leah and Darin's friends combined people from Darin's office and Leah's and a few high school and college friends that had settled in the Twin Cities. Sam only knew a few of them by name, but they seemed like a friendly crowd over all. Leah drew close and whispered in Sam's ear. "Why didn't you bring Gary?"

"Kiss mine," Sam whispered back in the same pleasant tone.

Sam meandered through the crowd holding her drink, looking everyone over, pretending to be looking for someone. She noticed the angle of a chin, the slow curve of a long neck. The way one woman, wearing too much mascara, held her wineglass with both hands. Leah continued to greet people at the door, filling glasses and passing around hors d'oeuvres.

Sam felt a hand on her elbow. "Hello there, sexy thing." Darin was in top form. He brushed up behind her, slipping his hand from her elbow to her waist. "Knock out dress."

"Jesus, Darin. Knock it off. You're embarrassing me." Sam pushed his hand from her waist. "Can't you hold your liquor or what?"

"Sam, that's a damn unfriendly attitude to bring to a party. People are going to think you're a bitch. You should be aware of that." Darin smiled, his handsome white teeth filling the tan face. He was attractive, and he knew it. His blue eyes reminded Sam of the circle of color on a peacock feather. "You look dynamite," he said, flashing the winning smile.

Sam thought perhaps she was overreacting. She'd known Darin a long time. It wasn't like he was acting any differently. She relaxed. "Thanks. So, any handsome men you can introduce me to?" Sam raised her eyebrows playfully.

Darin took her right hand and raised it to his lips. He kissed her hand, all the time looking into her face. "Hello, my name is Darin and I would love to show you the rest of the condo. Have you seen the guest bedroom yet?"

Sam jerked her hand away, her face growing red. "Drop dead, you asshole. You're not funny, and I don't get off on your prepackaged charm. You're making a fool of yourself." Sam walked away, heading for the kitchen and another drink. She filled her glass with club soda, headed for the bathroom, locked the door behind her, and looked in the mirror, catching her breath. She was flushed. It wasn't the first time Darin had insinuated that she'd be better off having a go with him than not, but he usually laughed afterwards and tried to make it a big joke. He wanted to be the center of attention. He was the one that always had the parties and always told the jokes.

Sam pulled Leah's brush from the drawer and brushed through her long, wavy hair, counting to fifty, stalling before going back out.

Sam placed herself in the crowd, speaking with several people, explaining that she was a friend of Leah's. She was aware of her long earrings, brushing against the padded shoulders of her dress, sparkling. They were fun, like icicles dangling from her ears. They made her feel elegant.

Leah was giving someone a tour of the condo, showing them the closets and master bedroom and bath. Sam felt like someone was watching her. She glanced around the room and saw a man she'd never seen before. He was looking right at her and didn't look away. He had sandy hair and a mustache. Leaning against the wall by the bay window, holding a beer, he raised the bottle, as if to say hello. Sam smiled and looked away. She often stared at people, but they were rarely aware of her. She sipped her soda and looked for a way to escape.

Sam got a refill and met up with Leah. "Okay, Lee. Details. Who's the guy in the living room in the navy sweater and gray cords? The one with the mustache and the sculptured face?"

Leah laughed and raised her eyebrows. "My, it's been some time since I've seen you take such an active interest in more than the face. You mean you want a name? Well, let me see." Leah walked toward the living room and stuck her head in, looking around.

"Jesus, don't be so obvious," Sam said, frustrated.

"And flighty too. It must be serious lust. Adam Green. Darin plays racquetball with him. You want me to introduce you?"

Sam paused. "Not yet. But thanks for the information."

Sam filled her glass and walked back into the living room. She stood at the window for a long time looking out at the old-fashioned street lamps lining the sidewalk. The backdrop of downtown.

"Nice view," he said, walking up next to her. Sam turned around and smiled.

"Yes. The snow keeps everything so clean."

"I'm Adam Green. I don't know a soul here and thought I better start introducing myself."

Sam reached out her free hand. "Sam Ellings. Nice to meet you. Samantha," she added, picking up on the look on his face. "People call me Sam. It's not that my parents wanted a boy or anything. At least I don't think so."

They shook hands. "Do you know most of these people?" he asked.

"No. Leah's a good friend. I've met a lot of these folks before, but I couldn't introduce them because I'm awful with names. I'm good with faces and that's it. How do you know Leah and Darin?"

"Darin and I play racquetball. I met him at the club. I said I didn't have any plans for tonight, so he invited me, and here I am."

"New Year's is a good time to be at a party." The noise level in the room was growing louder. Leah had turned up the music and people were shouting over it, the alcohol dulling their inhibitions.

"Do you need another drink?" Adam asked. "I'm going for one myself. I'd be glad to get you one."

"Thanks. I'll have a scotch and water." Sam handed him her glass. His hands were large. Long, thick fingers. He smiled and turned away with the glasses. Blue eyes. Or green. Sam made a mental note to keep herself in check. This guy might be attached or even married. She wanted to slow down. No one-night romance this New Year's Eve. Never again.

"AND AFTER I saw the bear in camp, I made sure we stored the food well above our heads." Adam was talking about a trip to Alaska that he'd taken the summer before.

"It sounds wonderful. I'd love to take a trip like that." The two were sitting on the captain's bench in the entry-way. It was near midnight. Adam kept looking at his watch.

"I'll go get us some champagne, so we have something to toast with. How's that?"

Sam smiled. "Fabulous." She'd been sitting with an empty glass for the past hour, listening, talking, absorbing the lines around his eyes. The prominent forehead. When he returned with the glasses, they sat down, facing each other again.

"We've got one minute." Adam smiled. "Ready to welcome the new year?"

"Sure." Sam nodded. "It could be a good one."

The guests all started the countdown at thirty seconds. Shouting people filled the room. When the confetti started flying, Adam put his hand on the back of Sam's neck, and they kissed for a long time. Sam backed away far enough to look at his face. "Are you attached?" she asked.

"I don't think so, but I feel pretty good about that kiss."

"No. I mean, to anyone else? I just want to know."

"Will you kiss me again if I'm not?"

"Absolutely." Sam leaned toward him again. After a couple of kisses and a toast, Sam looked around the room to wish Leah a Happy New Year. She saw Darin across the living room, on the sofa with some brunette woman, engaged in a smothering kiss. He seemed oblivious to the surroundings.

"Shit," Sam said.

"What's wrong?"

"Ah, I have to check on Leah. I'll talk to you in a little bit, okay?"

"Sure, I'll be here."

SAM FOUND Leah in the guest bedroom. She was standing looking into the mirror, her hands resting on the dresser. The room was dark. Sam walked in and closed the door. "Leah?"

She didn't answer, but brushed the back of her hand across her cheek. Sam came up behind her and put her hands on Leah's shoulders. "Ah Lee. What's going on? Are you okay?"

Leah forced a laugh. "Happy New Year, Sam. It is

past midnight, isn't it? I heard everyone screaming out there."

"What's going on, Lee?"

"Darin's trying to get into anybody's pants he can. That's what's going on. When I told him he was making a fool of himself, he told me to mind my own business. He said he was tired of me trying to run his life. Whatever that means. Boy, is he tanked."

"That jerk. Don't let him get away with it, Leah. He deserves to show you some respect. And if he can't do that, screw him, Tell him to get lost."

Leah shrugged. "I love him. I do. I just feel so damn dumb with everyone here and him running around like a sex-starved baboon." She stopped for a moment. "But, it'll be okay. It always is. You just go have fun."

"Oh screw that noise, Leah. Now come on; you come out with me too. What if I said something to him?"

"No. Not when he's been drinking like this. Just let it wear off." She dried her eyes with a tissue. "Great party, huh? Some hostess."

"Everything's fine out there, except that jerk. He's got a lot of apologizing to do tomorrow."

"Oh, he'll have a lot of I'm sorry lines. I might have them memorized. But he's a good guy. He just can't hold his liquor."

Sam gave Leah a hug. "Well, I hope the new year is a good one. I love you, lady."

"Happy New Year, Sam." Leah turned on the light and wiped the mascara from under her eyes. "So, did you meet Mr. Gorgeous?"

"Yeah. Some Happy New Year kiss."

"Well, get back there, you fool! He can't leave without your phone number."

"Thanks."

Sam walked back to the entryway where Adam was still sitting. "882-0088."

"Pardon me?" he said, standing up.

"My telephone number. 882-0088."

Adam smiled. "Eight o'clock Saturday. Where should I pick you up?"

"Thirty-four sixteen Girard. Second floor." She liked this game. "Jeans?"

"Fine. I'll look forward to it." He kissed her on the forehead and walked out to get his coat. Sam was still on the bench when he came back. "See you Saturday if I remember that address." He winked and backed out the front door.

## 15

After watering Alex, Sam pulled on two pairs of gray wool socks and her boots, grabbed her coat and backpack, and left the apartment. The sidewalks were shoveled most of the way, making a maze of snow piled waist high on each side. The sun was loud in an empty bowl of sky.

She got to ChoiceCare about one o'clock. The Christmas decorations were still dangling from the light poles and banisters of the front entryway. Rudolph perched precariously in a dirty drift of snow near the center of the yard. A plywood Santa stood at his side, cheeks and nose appropriately rosy in the cold air.

"Afternoon," she said to the nurse at the front desk. The woman glanced up through bifocals and nodded.

"How was your Christmas, Sam?" she called after her, almost as an afterthought.

Sam made an "okay" sign with her fingers and turned the corner. They had papered the hallway in a forest green print to match the pine carpeting. It smelled like paste and antiseptic. Old flowers. Sam knocked on Netty's door. "It's me, Netty."

"Come in, dear."

Sam hugged the old woman, sitting in a rocker near the window. Netty was small, her pale porcelain skin covering fine bones. A white braid hung down her back almost two feet. "Hi, Netty! I hope Santa was good to you." Sam pulled out a small gift and handed it to Netty. "Merry Belated Christmas!"

Netty smiled, opening the natural bristle brush, admiring its fine wood handle. "I didn't think they made them like this anymore. This should last me a good ten years. Thank you dear. It's lovely." She stood up, walked over to the bedside stand, and pulled a box out of the bottom drawer. "For you."

Sam opened the box as Netty stood over her. "It's my old coffee mill. It's an antique now, I guess. Just like me." She laughed.

Sam pulled the grinder out of the box. "How nice, a hand-powered one! Thanks, Netty. I like fresh coffee, but refuse to buy one of those obnoxious little electric things to grind it up."

"Well, I figured you'd enjoy it, and it was just sitting

in a box in my son's basement. Here. Sit down. How were your holidays?"

"Okay. Different, I didn't go home. I spent Christmas Eve with my boss and his family."

"Who?"

"Bart. At the frame shop."

"Why?"

"I didn't want to go home. Too much work. It doesn't seem worth it anymore."

"It happens."

"I told them I had to work late Christmas Eve, and I was tired. They understand that. Christmas is busy for them, too." Sam paused. "It was nice to be with Bart's family. He has kids. His wife is fun. We sang carols and drank hot cider. Real Norman Rockwell stuff."

"Jack Harris down in 208 passed on the night after Christmas. You drew him once, didn't you?" Netty pulled her braid around over her shoulder and began fingering it like a rosary.

"Didn't he play the piano?"

"That's him. Poor soul. But he hasn't been the same since his stroke. It might be for the best."

"How's Mildred been since her surgery?" Sam walked over to the shelf near the sink and got a small tin. She sat down, opened it up and began eating the mints inside.

"Just fine. Can see clear as a bell now. But enough

about all us old geezers. How are you doing? You met a nice young man, didn't you?"

"What makes you say that?" Sam smiled. Her entire face reacted.

"When you've been around as long as I have, Samantha, you notice how every part of the body speaks. You've been telling me about it ever since you walked in."

"I want to hear more about this, as an artist. I want to know this language!"

"Your hands and feet gave you away first. Moving all the time. And swinging your hair off your shoulders. When you're unhappy, you let things settle in. So, is this something I get to hear about?"

"Absolutely. But it's not much yet. I mean, I met him on New Year's Eve, and we have a date on Tuesday. Oh, God, why do I do this to myself? I swear Netty, I never learn."

"You learn, dear, just very slowly. Love is work. You need to be willing to take risks. You can do that, can't you?"

Sam reached across the table and covered Netty's small hand. "I will never be as brave as you are, but I guess I'll give this another try. It's only a first date. What can it hurt?"

"What's his name?"

"Adam."

"Hmmm. An old name. That's nice."

Sam smiled. "He's nice. Do you mind if I sketch a little? You look stunning right now in that light."

Netty ran her hand down her braid. "Under one condition. You stay for a game of pinochle."


NETTY PICKED up the Jack of Diamonds and laid down her hand. "You know, your Grandma used to beat me regularly at cards." She chuckled; her shoulders shaking. "It doesn't look like you've got her touch, Sam. That's three games in a row."

Sam sat with her stocking feet up on Netty's bed. "I never could beat her either, but then, she never beat me at tennis. Keep that in mind."

Netty shuffled the cards and put them back in the box. "I can just see Amanda out there on the tennis court with her cane in one hand and a racquet in the other." Her hands shook like leaves teased in a soft breeze. "Your Gran might actually have tried something like that."

"I remember we went snowmobiling once at home. She had to be near seventy. It was after that first surgery. Anyway, she climbed on behind me, and we rode for an hour and a half along the river." Sam tossed her head back. "God, she was screaming at the top of her lungs. 'Faster! Let's go a little faster.' I couldn't believe it."

Netty got up slowly and walked over to the thermostat, putting her face close to the dial to read it. "Are you getting chilly? I think it's a little chilly."

"Do you miss her much, Netty? I know I do."

Netty filled the electric teapot at the small sink in the corner and plugged it in. "Sure, dear. I miss her. I miss lots of people. It's like I have two lives, the one I'm living here and the one I'm remembering every day." Sam stared out the window, white with frost at the corners. "My memories reach back a long way."

The room was filling with shadows as dusk settled on the snow outside. Lights turned on in the hallway. A vacuum cleaner growled at the end of the corridor. Sam reached over and pulled the chain on the bedside lamp. The shade was made of four cardboard egg carton separators, spray painted gold. A marble was glued in each indentation. The light showed through the colored swirls. The final touch was a border of red pompoms trimming the bottom of the shade.

"I miss her too." Sam said, her depressed mood jarred by the garish light fixture. She had the urge to laugh. "Netty, where did you get this lamp?"

"Mildred brought it over. She has about six of them in her room and needed to find space for a new potted geranium her son gave her. It's a little loud, don't you think?"

"Oh, perhaps just a little." Sam flicked a finger at one pompom. "Did that guy move out next door? It looked empty as I came in."

"Died. Stroke. Both he and his wife now in three months. Some go like that."

A cart rattled down the hall, glassware bouncing along. "Sounds like dinner, Netty. I'd better get going. You need anything from the store? I could drop some things by tomorrow."

"No, dear. I'm fine. You'll have to come by next week, though. We're having a big bingo tournament. We invite guests and the prizes are pretty big. One hundred dollars a game is the rumor. Some big company donated money. You could use a hundred dollars, couldn't you?" An aide brought in a tray of food.

"Sure could. Smells like fish and broccoli," Sam said. She kissed Netty on the forehead. "Have a wonderful dinner. Thanks for the coffee mill." The teapot whistled as she was leaving the room.

Sam walked back home, listening to the snow crunch beneath her boots. The temperature was dropping. Tern's corner grocery store had added a green neon sign in the window, keeping up with the flashy new businesses in Uptown. With four lakes close by, snuggled into the heart of south Minneapolis, the climate was perfect for development. The hardware store lost its lease, and yogurt and bagel shops took over. Then the fancy mall came in, and before long, every restaurant and cafe was putting tables out on the sidewalk, and Uptown was the place to be seen. At least that was true in the summer. Sam liked the area. In the summer she could watch people and in the winter she could see how the same people dressed to stay warm: mufflers wrapped around faces, chopper mittens, down coats, wool socks. Thinsulate. The language of Minnesotans.

When she got home, Sam turned on all the lights in her small apartment. The dry Christmas tree still stood in the corner of the living room, needles scattered beneath it.

## 16

"**A**re you going to show me the apartment, or are we leaving?" Adam stood at the top of the stairs, snow caked to the bottoms of his jeans. Sam held a brush in her hand and ran through her hair one more time. "If we are going," he continued, "I'd suggest you grab some shoes. There's a good three feet of snow out there."

Motioning for Adam to come into the living room, Sam went to get her hiking boots. She called from the bedroom. "I've lived here a long time. I'm just not one for a lot of furniture, but have a chair, or a futon, I should say. I'm almost ready to go." She glanced in the mirror; the emerald sweater accented her eyes. When she came back out, Adam had unfolded the lawn chair and was reclining, holding a contented dog on his lap.

. . .

"I LIKE YOUR PLACE. Is all of this artwork yours?"

Sam pushed up the sleeves on her thick sweater. "Yeah. My only gallery these days. I pay the rent, so I figure I'll display all that I can."

"It's nice. I'd like to see more."

"Another time, okay?" Sam grabbed her stomach. "I'm starved!"

Adam looked a little embarrassed. "I'm sorry. I should have made it a little later or earlier?"

She shrugged. "It's okay. I'm teasing. I'm always hungry."

"But, I've already eaten." Adam looked serious.

"That's all right," Sam answered, not missing a beat. "You can just buy me dinner then."

Adam laughed. "I haven't eaten, but I'm going to have to work to catch you off guard. I can see that. Like Vietnamese food?"

"You bet. I may as well tell you now; food is one of my hobbies. I enjoy almost any kind of food. The world is my restaurant, you might say." She patted Alex and filled up his water bowl. "Ready when you are."

THEY ATE AT PERFUME RIVER, a small restaurant on the west bank of the Mississippi near the University. It was busy and brightly lit, the atmosphere plain and unassuming. Sam noticed the waitress's small hands and thin wedding band. She wore support hose and black work shoes with thick soles. The front window was steamy and clouded. The peach and yellow neon sign cast a bland blanket of warm light. Sam glanced at Adam and saw he was staring at her. "I'm sorry, I've been rude," she said. "I have a habit of soaking up my surroundings, sometimes at my company's expense."

"Your subjects?"

She nodded.

"See anything promising?"

"Yes, actually. There's a boy near the back that has his legs wrapped around the legs of his chair. Quite a talent. And there's this man that's having some kind of affair with his eyeglasses, keeps cleaning them with his napkin. I swear he's cleaned them at least four times. And there's one guy with the greatest eyes." Sam paused. "I'd like to get a chance to draw him."

Adam shrugged. "Go give him your card; he'll think you're making a pass, but he has to pay for both our dinners if you end up with a date out of this."

"Well, I don't have a card, but I'll see what I can do." Sam reached into her bag and brought out a small notebook. She jotted something on it. "Sir, I'm sorry if I've been staring at you, but I'm rather taken with your forehead and eyes, and well, the general layout of your face, I was wondering if sometime it might be possible to have you sit for me... so that I could sketch you?" She smiled and slid the paper across the table to him.

Adam read out loud. "Sam Ellings. Artist at large. What's in it for me?"

Sam shrugged her shoulders. "Cheesecake?"

"Cheesecake?"

"Yeah, next Saturday night, at my apartment. After a dinner, of course. And a couple-hour sitting. I make a great cheesecake."

"It sounds okay, but I warn you. I can't even stand still for a photo. I wouldn't be a good subject."

"Oh, you'll be great." Sam winked.

"It sounds like we have another date, then." Adam said.

"Huh, imagine that. And I even swung that one, didn't I? Boy, I'm clever," Sam replied.



"Is THERE any significance to the name of this place?" Sam asked the waitress when she brought their egg rolls.

The woman pulled a pencil out from behind her ear and lifted her hair up with the eraser, playing with it. "It's a river in Vietnam, I guess. That's about all I know."

"Thanks." Sam dipped a crispy roll into the small white porcelain cup of hot sauce, turning back to Adam. "Stellar name. If I were in a rock band, I'd call it Perfume River."

Adam took a slow bite, chewing and staring at the front door. "It's strange what Vietnam means ten, fifteen years later." He looked at Sam and smiled. "Restaurants and egg rolls."

"Were you over there?" Sam's brow furrowed.

"No." Adam took a sip of tea. "I had a college deferment and a bad knee." He stopped. Looked out somewhere past Sam. "My twin brother had a different view. He wanted to go. Thought he might be a career man. Couldn't see himself in law school or medical school or any school, for that matter. He wanted action."

"You have a twin! Wow! That must be neat. Is he? A career man, I mean?"

"No." Adam's face was full of indecision. A wrinkled brow. Eyes traveling again. "He was killed. Three months in Nam. A couple letters home and he was gone."

"Oh, God." Sam's throat constricted. She couldn't swallow. "God, I'm sorry. I'm so sorry."

Adam sighed and reached for her hand. "It was a long time ago, and I've settled up with it. We don't need to talk about it. Sometimes it just hits again, and I start comparing. Sorry I brought it up."

Sam looked at the iceberg lettuce cradling her appetizer. She looked at his hand around hers. She wanted to keep those fingers, to take his hand home with her; she wanted something to hold on to.

. . .

THEY WALKED to a nearby bar and had a couple drinks while they listened to a jazz ensemble. The effects of the alcohol in the warm bar loosened Sam up, and she started asking questions. "I don't even know what you do for a living. You live on Lake Minnetonka, and you like to cross-country ski, but I never even asked what you do! All I've been talking about is my work, my this, my that. Jesus Christ."

"DON'T GET TOO upset about it. At least I know you're not after me for my money," Adam said, a smirk on his face.

"God, don't tell me you have money. I'll get real nervous, and I'm sure I won't say the right things, and I couldn't possibly be having such a great time with somebody with a lot of cash."

"Just like an artist to stereotype. I never said I had a lot. I just said you weren't after me for my money, and you're breaking off the relationship before we even get a good kiss in. Well, besides the ones on New Year's Eve, but that could have been social pressure. I'm just not sure what to think of this whole thing, Samantha." He was raising his voice and waving his arms around. A waiter stopped and turned to look. Sam laughed.

"Okay. I give. I give. Tell me more; tell me everything. I'll still make cheesecake. I'll let you sit on my lawn chair, pet my dog, anything. I guess I can draw a rich guy; it might be a new artistic challenge."

"Jesus." Adam rolled his eyes, a smile forcing wrinkles at the corners. "I'm not sure this is the right time to be telling our life stories. Somehow the mood seems too bazaar."

"Sure it is, look." Sam leaned over the table and took his hand. "My parents own Ellings furniture store near St. Cloud. I wore braces for four-and-a-half years, and people at school called me tinsel teeth. In junior high, I was sure I would never get boobs, and I almost burned our kitchen down once when I was trying to make candles. When I was in college, I loved to go skinny dipping in the rock quarries." She paused for breath. "See? Now that's my past. Should I tell you anything about the present?"

"No, thanks. I'd like to find that out for myself. It feels like I just read the Reader's Digest version of your teenage diaries. Okay, Let's see. I have a dog too."

"Really?" Sam interrupted. "I should have known; you were so nice to Alex. What kind?"

"Samantha. You talk too much." Adam squeezed her hand.

"Somebody else told me that, believe it or not." Sam twirled her ice cubes around in the empty glass. "Now, you were talking about your dog?"

Adam shook his head. Sam stared at his smiling face. Sharp features. Strength and playfulness.

"Lady's a retriever. Ever since I was a little boy and saw that movie Lady and the Tramp, I wanted a dog named Lady. At home I never got to name the dogs, so she was my first chance." Adam ordered another round. "I have a lot of land for her to run on. It's a nice place. You'll have to come and see it. My practice is right on the property, so I don't have to go far to work."

"Practice?" Sam asked.

"I'm a vet. Mostly small domestic animals, but I also see a lot of horses. There are plenty of stables in the area."

"Dr. Green!" Sam said with emphasis. "Then you do have money. Oh, god. Well, anyway, I'm impressed."

"Don't be. It's just a job. People always get impressed by titles, but I do like my work, and I don't tire of working with animals."

"I love animals. I'd like to see your place, I mean, the animals…" Sam stumbled a little, embarrassed. She was staring into Adam's eyes, and he was staring right back. She caught her breath. Something told her to keep things under control, but she barely listened to the noises.

BACK AT SAM'S APARTMENT, they stood on the steps. "Then can I expect you for dinner next Saturday? Can you come in the middle of the afternoon so the light will be good for drawing?" Sam wanted to keep talking and looking at him. "I need some of the natural light, and it would be best..."

"What are you doing Thursday? How about some cross-country skiing out by my place? There should be a moon. It's beautiful along the lake. I noticed you have skis."

"I work at the frame shop until 4:00, so I'd be home after that. That would be great. I..." She paused and smiled. "Happy New Year." She shrugged her shoulders.

He leaned forward and whispered, "Happy New Year" before he kissed her.

## 17

Sunday morning, Sam was leaving the apartment when the phone rang. Rexel didn't bother with hello. "I'm going on a plane. On vacation to the Bahamas. That's an island. And I might get to go... Sam?"

Sam laughed. "Hi, Rexel. What's all this about?"

"Mom's taking me on a trip for ten days. We're going to this island, and I get to go swimming in the ocean."

"Great! When?"

"Tomorrow or something. I've never been on a plane. I get out of school for ten days."

"That's wonderful! Have fun and send me a post-card." Rexel had never called before. "Stop and see me when you get back. I'd like to hear about it. You going to work on getting a good tan?" She teased, almost as an afterthought.

Rexel was silent at first, taken aback, but eventually a sigh and a small laugh escaped. "You're so weird, Sam. Have fun in the cold."

SAM MET Leah at a cafe in Uptown for a late breakfast. They shopped at a secondhand store afterwards, trying on old chiffon dresses and oversized men's suite coats. Sam bought a black Derby, pulling it down to her ears as they walked down toward the lake.

It was a cloudless morning without a wind. The snow crunched under their feet. The lake lay like a huge frisbee in the middle of south Minneapolis. Fish houses stood spattered across the north end. Sam and Leah reached the plowed path around the lake for die hard joggers and walkers. Most of them wore wool scarves wrapped around their faces. One man had icicles hanging down over his neck, filling his beard.

"So the date was all right, huh?" Leah smiled and glanced over at Sam. They had already discussed it over breakfast.

"Above average," Sam replied. "I'd say definitely above average."

Leah zipped her coat the last few inches to her neck. "Want to go to New Orleans or something? How about Houston? We need to go on a vacation; It's too damn cold here."

Sam remembered Rexel's call. "I could see it. Let's go to an island somewhere. How about Jamaica? We could sit and listen to Jamaican music and soak up the sun."

"Fine, except you can't drive to Jamaica. We could take the old Celica and hit the road. I could afford that. Airfare, I doubt. This furnishing the condo stuff is taxing on the credit cards."

"If you're talking realism here, we may as well discuss southern warm weather locations like Sioux City or Omaha. My cash supply is real low."

"What about in a couple of months? I'm serious. We could drive down to the gulf and spend a couple of days. You could get a week off, couldn't you? God, it would do me good to get away. I'm sick of this town. I'm sick of Minnesota. Hell, the whole Midwest has lost its appeal to me."

Sam thought about it. "How about in March? I bet I could swing a couple hundred by March. How much would it cost us?"

"Wouldn't it be nice? A beach and a cool drink. No jobs, no hassles, and no snow. We have gone nowhere together since our sophomore year, when we spent spring break in Daytona."

"I'll have to talk to Bart at work. I'll check it out." Four feet high drifts of snow stood on both sides of the path, making it look like a white hedge. A woman passed with a small poodle on a leash. The dog looked both ways, as if looking for a doorway out of the walls of snow.

## 18

An orange moon dangled between two slender, colorless tree trunks. Sam stopped and leaned on her ski pole to catch her breath. Adam glanced back at the next curve and stopped, waiting for her to catch up. The snow cover was thick; airy flakes powdered old ski ruts. Sam had a little trouble seeing the path ahead of her.

She skied ahead and stopped behind Adam. "You have one long trail here. Does the Olympic team train on your property or something?"

He smiled. "Only when I give them permission. How about some hot chocolate by the fireplace? There's a shortcut back."

"Wonderful. I'll follow you."

A bright, spirited fire was lighting the living room by the time Adam returned with the steaming milk. Sam had taken off her sweat socks and was warming her toes by the hearth. She looked around at the leather furniture, the brass, and glass. Enormous windows faced the frozen lake. Stark drifts, moonlight, and miles of snow. "This is an incredible place. I can't believe this house and that you live here alone."

Adam settled down on the plush carpet next to her and handed her a cup. "You can't believe you like someone who has money. You said so yourself, but you can relax; I have a mortgage like everybody else."

Sam leaned her head back on a pile of pillows. "Are you a Republican?"

"God, Sam, you stereotype so easily. I'm not sure I like that about you."

"Then you are a Republican?"

"If I am, are you going to stop seeing me?" He was teasing now.

"I might. I'd definitely consider it."

"Yeah, let's face it. We don't have a thing in common; we shouldn't be starting a relationship." Adam pulled the hair off Sam's neck and began kissing her. "I don't know much about art, and you don't know much about anything."

She loved the games; the witty little hills and curves in their conversations. She turned to sass back, but he interrupted her with a long kiss. Nothing mattered then; save the smooth curve of his neck in her palm and the warm energy like corn popping in the pit of her stomach.

When the fire died down, Adam took her hand, and they walked into his bedroom.

"REPUBLICAN, USUALLY." Adam said. Sam stirred, disoriented. She had been sleeping in a tangle of sheets. The room was unfamiliar. A candle flickered on a table by the bed. Adam was sitting on top of the covers, a tray of bread, cheese, and cold cuts in front of him. He uncorked a bottle of wine.

"Huh?" Sam's voice was husky with sleep.

"My party preference. Now you know. I needed a midnight snack. It's one of my few flaws. I get hungry at night. You like mustard on your sandwiches?"

Sam looked at the bedside clock. It was 3:30. "Oh, that looks so good. I'm pretty sure if I wasn't asleep, I'd be starved. Give me sixty seconds."

Leaning against several pillows, sheets pulled up under her arms, Sam bit into a hard roll. "You have found the direct route to my heart. I grant you three wishes."

"I didn't want to waste any of this time with you sleeping. I want to stay awake with you for the rest of the night." They drank wine and nibbled at the food. Four long windows faced the lake in this room as well. The view was spectacular. An eerie blue light from the almost-full moon illuminated the trees near the shore, the boathouse, and the deck behind the house.

"How long have you lived here?"

"Three years. I started my practice five years ago and moved it out here when I got the property."

"Is your family rich too?"

"My father's doing okay. He sells tractors and other machinery in the southern part of the state, and Mom teaches high school up in Alexandria."

"Divorced?"

"Yeah. After Aaron was killed in Vietnam, they sort of fell apart. Just the time they needed to lean on each other for support, they decided they didn't love each other anymore. They divorced within a year. It was almost like they couldn't be reminded of what life was like before."

"Did you regret not being in Vietnam? I mean, not fighting?"

"Sure. Guilt's a partner to grief. Oh, I was pretty pissed off with God. I figured he could have left Aaron alone and wiped me out in a car accident or something. Some kind of swap. But the prayers started echoing pretty quickly, and I felt like I was talking to myself."

Sam shook her head. "I can't imagine being so close like that and..."

Adam put the tray of food on the floor and blew out the candle. He reached over and pulled Sam close, cradling her head on his shoulder. "I can't explain that war, and I can't explain the loss, but I learned to remember. I don't want to forget a thing."

The two lay in the bed, shadowed by bright moonlight. Sounds danced around the house, and Sam listened intently for a long time. The refrigerator hummed and clicked off. The alarm clock ticked out a comforting rhythm. Adam finally relaxed, his shoulder muscles melting beneath her arm. His breathing was soft and steady, the pattern of sleep.

Sam woke up to the sound of an electric shaver in the adjoining bathroom. Closing her eyes, she stretched her arms above her head. A smile pulled at the corners of her mouth. Usually, in the morning, the memory of passion seemed less than real; she was sure the warm feelings would disappear when he hadn't called for four or five days, when he told her the relationship was going too fast, when some dusty old photograph entered the picture again. She was familiar with all the stage directions for that scene.

Adam stood in the doorway, a towel wrapped around his waist. "Morning. I have to be in the office by ten, so we can catch a quick breakfast here, and I'll take you in. What time do you have to be at work?"

Sam glanced at the bedside clock. "It doesn't matter. You can just drop me off at home. I need to let Alex out. That would be fine." She smiled at Adam and yawned.

Already her stomach was sending nervous signals back and forth to her brain. She sat up and pulled the sheets around her. Adam disappeared back into the bathroom and came out wearing jeans and a sweater. He rubbed a towel in his wet hair.

The room smelled like shampoo and shaving cream. "Want to shower? I'll make breakfast."

The bathroom was enormous. Maroon and gray tile. Rows of bright lights. A stack of plush white towels near the shower. Sam smelled his cologne. She looked in the mirror and saw herself, hair messed and the rosy color of sleep still on her cheeks. There were mirrors in front and behind her; mirrors and money everywhere.

## 19

The evening news was on when the telephone rang. "Sam? It's me." Leah sounded close to tears, tired. "I want to come over. That asshole. Are you home? I mean, are you going to be home?"

"Leah? Are you all right? Sure, come on over. Have you eaten? I'll put some dinner on." Leah had already hung up. Sam held the receiver and realized that Leah may have been drinking. She redialed her number, but heard only a steady line of rings.

She walked into the kitchen to put on coffee, acting out of habit. Sam struck a match and held the blue flame to the front burner of the range. Her hand was shaking. It was only about two-and-a-half miles. Leah would be okay. Maybe she wasn't drinking. She was upset, that was all. "Damn, Darin." She started water for the coffee and browned some hamburger for spaghetti. The smell of the hot fat hung over the small kitchen.

At seven o'clock, Sam had chopped every onion and pepper in the house. Sauce was spattering on the back burner, dotting the white enamel of the stove with oily orange spots. Sam paced the floor. "So, she stopped off somewhere. She'll be here, or she'll call. Leah, God damn it, call."

She heard the crash. It sounded as if it had happened right outside her window. A horn blared one long note. Sam put on her jacket as she ran down the stairs.

The night was hollow and cold. A broad circle of yellow light surrounded the street lamp in front of the house. It was snowing. When Sam reached the sidewalk, she could see the two cars in the middle of the intersection, one horn echoing in the darkness.

The smaller car's blinker was flashing; its front end twisted in on itself. It was Leah's blue Toyota Celica. "Lee..." Sam's voice was a weak whisper as she ran into the intersection. People were already standing in their doorways. "Call an ambulance," she screamed. "Somebody get help!"

Sam moved out of her body and took herself by the hand. Two men in parkas were attending to the other car. She pulled at Leah's door, but it resisted. She put one foot on the car, pulled again, and it opened. Leah was slumped over the steering wheel and wasn't moving.

Bleeding, breathing, poison. Sam recalled every detail of her college first aid course. Don't move the victim. Keep them warm. There was warm moisture on Leah's head. It was dark, except for the lights from the dash. She groped for the inside lights. "Leah, are you okay? Come on, Lee, talk to me. It's Sam."

She found the knob and turned it. Light flooded the car. Broken glass and rust red blood covered the seat, covered Leah's blond hair. Sam smelled whiskey and turned off the light, taking short, shaky breaths. "Leah, listen to me. I don't know what to do and you've got to stop bleeding, hear me?"

Cradling her head, Sam leaned Leah back on the seat. The sudden silence from the horn's release startled Sam. She thought she had killed her friend. She leaned back out of the car and stood for a moment, big flakes of snow falling all around her. Turn on the light. Forget the blood. Stop the red from coming. A long gash in Leah's forehead bled profusely. Sam held her palm directly over the cut to slow the oozing blood. She looked for other cuts, but it was so hard to tell. Sam put two fingers on Leah's neck. There was a pulse, and she was breathing; it was just all that blood.

Soon, a rescue squad arrived in the middle of spinning red lights. Sam didn't hear the sirens until they parked right next to the car. Two paramedics pulled her away. Questions from somewhere. Cold hands. Her face was wet. She rode with Leah in the ambulance to the hospital.

Outside the ambulance, huge flakes of snow filled the air. An orange city truck spreading sand on the street pulled over as they passed. Blue lights flashing. Red, yellow, green. Emergency. White light. "Please come this way."


THE WAITING room was quiet except for the soft hum of a flickering florescent light. It was 11:30 p.m.; they moved Leah to Intensive Care as a precaution. She'd broken a couple of ribs, her collarbone, and her right arm. There was some internal bleeding, and she'd had surgery. They stitched her face up, and she was sleeping. Sam didn't know the rest.

She called Leah's mother in St. Cloud, but she was still on vacation. Leah's grandma would call her in Phoenix and let her know. Sam stood up and then sat down again on the blue sofa. Everything was geometric. Blue and green carpeting squares gave way to long strips of one color. Follow the blue hallway to information, the green hallway to the cafeteria, and the elevators for floors two through seven.

She didn't know who to call. The air was stale and smelled of antiseptic and cigarette ashes. A small Vietnamese woman holding her rounded belly smiled and walked past her to the green hallway. A man followed her, carrying an overnight bag.

Sam couldn't go home. She couldn't be any more alone than this. She went to the reception counter. "Excuse me, is it possible to see her? Just for a few minutes? I understand I'm not family, but they can't get here. Couldn't you ask her doctor or something?" The woman behind the counter smiled and explained the policy again. There was no news yet. In the morning. Perhaps in the morning.

Sam walked back to the sofa, and then to the telephone. It was almost one o'clock. She looked up Adam's number and dialed. It rang several times before a sleepy voice answered.

"Adam? Hi." Tears ran down Sam's cheeks to her chin.

"I'm sorry. It's late."

"Sam?" Adam's voice grew clear and alert. "Are you okay?"

"No. I, ah...I need you." The sobs came then, rolling out into the empty room. Sam needed to make it clear, to tell the story. She took a deep breath, calling back the gasps. "I'm at Woodbridge General Hospital. Leah's been in an accident, and I can't see her, and she's in ICU, and I don't know if she's going to be okay, and I'm terrified. Could you, could you please come down here? I'm sorry.

I know it's late." Sam paused. "I didn't know who to call."

"Sam, just sit down, and I'll be right there." Adam sounded stern, yet comforting. "Do you hear me? I'll be there as soon as I can."

"Thanks." Sam hung up the phone and followed the blue hallway to the drinking fountain. Maybe it was her fault. She should have guessed Leah was drinking. She should have called someone. But who? For the first time, she remembered Darin. She walked back to the phone and dialed Leah's and Darin's number, but there was no answer.

The halls were quiet. Nurses joked quietly at the desk and talked about a TV show. Sam memorized the covers of magazines on the table in front of her. TIME. NEWSWEEK. NEW WOMAN. Reagan and Bush. Cher. Diets. Hairdos. Holiday food.

ADAM CAME and took her home. There wasn't any more she could do at the hospital until morning. Leah's mother would fly in tomorrow. Adam had asked around and Leah was resting and out of critical condition. She was out of danger.

When they reached Sam's apartment, she smelled the old hamburger as soon as she opened the door at the bottom of the stairs. Alex went into a frenzy when he saw her. Adam took him outside. Sam shuddered and ran upstairs to the bathroom and threw up until all she had left in her was dry, demanding heaves.

Adam came in and turned on the faucets in the tub. He poured bath crystals into the water and the perfumed suds covered the stale odor of tomato sauce in the air. Sam was still chilled from the drive; it was fifteen degrees below zero outside. Warm steam misted over the window as Sam slid down along the wall to the floor.

"Come here." Adam had taken off his coat and rolled up the sleeves of his flannel shirt. He gently helped Sam get off her coat and boots. "I think a bath would be a good idea. Is that okay?" His voice was slow and steady. Sam's muscles began to relax.

"Both of us? I don't think there's room." She smiled.

"I've had mine, thank you." He unbuttoned her blouse and slipped it off her bare shoulders. It fell around her waist. He took her hands and helped her to her feet. Sam slipped out of her jeans and underwear and hugged him; her slim pale body against all that fabric. His belt buckle was cold on her stomach; it was good to feel again.

Adam washed her body; the warm, sudsy sponge taking all the shattered glass out of the night. He talked about his camping trip to Alaska, about comfortable things like starting camp fires and getting water from fresh streams. "I drove up with a good friend from college, and this one day we stopped at some natural hot springs. You had to walk in about a mile on these little one-by-twelve planks because it was so swampy, and we wondered if there was a hot spring at all because we didn't meet anyone on the path. Anyway, our guidebook listed it, so we were determined to find it. Then it was right there. No hoopla, no little buildings, and tourist traps, just two huge aqua steaming pools. The water was so hot it turned my legs red in seconds, but once I got used to it, it felt great. It was so strange, being out in the middle of the forest, the air cool and wet. We sat there in this spa like kings. Nobody showed up the whole time we were there. You had to get out of the water and walk around about every five minutes or else your legs just refused to work." Adam massaged Sam's shoulders. "Pretty relaxing stuff. You'd like it."

Sam leaned into his hands and relaxed. "Do me a favor?" she said. "Will you throw out that food?" She stayed in the water for almost an hour, listening to sounds from the kitchen and the sound of bubbles as they disappeared.

## 20

Thursday morning Sam bought a bouquet of balloons in the hospital gift shop and took them up to Leah's room, where she was watching a soap opera, her face bruised and bandaged, deep black circles under her eyes. Leah looked at the balloons and back at the television. "Are those for you or me?"

Sam tied the strings on to the bed stand. "Both. We can split them up when I leave. How are you?"

"Ah, minus the broken bones and the headache, I feel like hell. How about you?"

Sam stood by the bed and reached out to Leah's fingers. "God, you scared me, lady. I mean it."

Leah blinked back tears. "It wasn't my night to go visiting, I guess." Sam carefully lifted a strand of hair away from her friend's forehead. She wanted to crawl up on the bed next to Leah and hold her, let her cry until it was over, until she could put it behind her, but something inside closed off. Sam only smiled.

"Darin left me," Leah said. "Just packed his little bag and said he'd see me around. He said I could have the apartment until the lease ran out. A going-away present, I suppose. How about that?" She tilted her chin up and looked at her friend.

Sam sat down in the chair by the bed. "Why?"

"Who knows? We didn't get personal about it. It wasn't what you'd call a long conversation."

"That jerk." Sam searched for words. There weren't any, and she knew it. She fingered the stiff white sheet next to her. "Well, the hell with him. Listen, I'll take care of your place, water your plants and stuff until you get out of here, and then we can have a party or something. Celebrate freedom. We could even go on that vacation and get some sun."

Leah clicked off the TV and closed her eyes. "Jesus, Sam. You can bug the crap out of me sometimes. You and your damn cheerful attitude. I am so tired of listening to you make jokes and try to laugh away everything that happens. I don't need it anymore. I don't need the way you cope; I don't need your jokes or your lectures..." She paused and opened her eyes... "In fact, I don't need you at all. So why don't you just bounce out of here right now?"

Sam stood up. "Leah, I understand this is hard, but you can get some help…"

"1 don't need any goddamn help!" she screamed. "I'll dry out without you and without him. Now get the hell out of my life!"

Sam felt the panic begin near the roof of her mouth and spread out to cover her throat. Her eyes blurred over. It was as if the inside of her body was fighting to get out, and she was about to explode. "I'm sorry…" She backed out of the room and stood in the hallway. "Leah, I..."

"Get out!"

Sam ran for the elevator, pushing the button several times. Finally, she took the stairs, gripping the railing and stumbling down flight after flight. She stopped in the lobby and sat down, gasping for breath.

"Sam?" Rexel stood in front of her.

Sam looked up, surprised, tears wetting her cheeks. "Rexel. What are you doing here?"

"It's my mom…" Rexel grabbed his companion's hand. "This is my aunt Helen. This is Sam."

"Hello." The woman looked suspiciously at Sam.

"Hello." Sam wiped her hand across her cheeks. "It's nice to meet you. Rexel, how was your vacation?"

"Are you all right?" Rexel asked.

Sam was shaking now. "You went to the Bahamas, didn't you?"

Rexel nodded. She took a deep breath. "Is your

mother okay?" Her voice broke at the end. She didn't want an answer. She couldn't handle an answer. Rexel just looked at the ground. Sam looked at her watch. "I'm sorry, I've got to go. Rexel, I'm sorry." She backed out the doors as they slid open for her. A blast of cold air hit her, stinging her wet cheeks. Snow was blowing around in the fierce gusty air, swirling, forming small whirlwinds on the sidewalk as Sam headed home.

## 21

Work took the rough edges off. Smoothed the wrinkles. The next several weeks passed as late winter can in Minnesota, one day like the next. Cold. White. Car exhaust escaping into the blue sky.

Sam found out from Darin that Leah entered treatment; Darin moved out while she was gone, leaving the designer towels and furniture. He sounded happy on the phone, but a little tired. It was a tiring time of year.

"I got a nice place near downtown. It's close to work. How are things with you and the doc?"

"When is Leah going home? Has she asked about me?"

"Look, Sam. Leah and I aren't on talking terms ourselves. Her mother called me. It all depends, I

144

suppose, on how she's doing. If I hear anything, I'll call you."

"Thanks. I appreciate it."

"I just couldn't take it anymore, you know? All the booze. The jealousy. It wasn't meant to work."

"I don't suppose. Work, I mean. That's what it ends up being, isn't it?"

"Well. You have my new number. I'll talk to you."

"Sure."

SAM AND ADAM sat on the living room floor with a pizza between them. "I used to be a vegetarian for about a year, but I missed pepperoni and sausage pizza." Sam took another slice and folded it in half. "Nothing quite substitutes for pepperoni."

"I was considering getting out of here and driving out to Colorado to do some skiing or flying somewhere warm. That sounds even better. I'm ready for a beach. Would you be interested in going along?"

Sam remembered Leah's plans for heading south together and Gary's invitation to Boston. She wanted to be the one to put her finger on the map for once and say where she was going to go. "I've got to work. I can't take a week right now."

"You need some time away. Wouldn't your boss understand?"

"Sure, but my landlord wouldn't. Look, it may be hard to understand, but I get by week to week, and I can't swing a vacation on that kind of cash flow."

"Well, that's no problem." Adam smiled. "I can pay for the trip, and if you need any more money, we'll just get you some. How's that?"

"No thanks, Santa." Sam's voice was cold and short.

"I didn't mean to offend you. Look, I'd like you to go somewhere with me, and I have plenty to cover it. Why does that have to be a problem?"

"Because you don't get it." Sam took a breath. "I appreciate the offer, but I don't want your money. I don't want to be indebted."

"It isn't a loan I'm talking about. I'd like to help. I'd like to have a little bigger part in your life."

"Well, you can't buy a share, okay? I knew this wouldn't work. I feel like some project of yours. We have nothing in common. I don't know what we're doing, anyway." Sam walked into the kitchen.

"Just passing time, I guess." Adam picked up his coat. He walked into the kitchen and leaned on the door frame. "I'm comfortable with who I am, Sam, and with who you are—but if you keep playing this Cinderella game, I don't see what comes next. Okay, you don't want or need my help. You don't need a vacation. You want some vision of the starving artist? You got it. But if your work mattered as much as your pride, you'd look twice at some of your choices." He zipped his coat. "I'm taking some time off. It will be good for me to rethink this thing too. Maybe we are running too fast in a dark alley. I don't know." He paused. "Call me sometime if you want to talk?"

Sam smiled. She felt the familiar panic of making decisions and then feeling like someone else had made them. She was already unsure of herself. "Send me a postcard?"

"Sure." Adam shrugged. He smiled and waved. The bell on the door at the bottom of the stairs broke the silence for a moment as he closed it behind him.

## 22

A dam likes to hunt. He collects old wooden duck decoys on shelves at the end of the living room. The display case is hand-crafted oak. One striking decoy belonged to his father. He gave it to Adam before the divorce. Adam told Sam this one evening as they sat in front of the fire. The gift duck is pointing out to the lake. Sam is dreaming this duck alive in the late night of her own bed.

Sam is sitting in Adam's living room. He is not there. It is not clear where he is. He might be out delivering some pups or with a sick horse. It doesn't matter. Sam is in the room alone, surrounded by leather and wood. She is thinking about art. In this dream, she had just sold an oil painting of a pair of scissors to the Metropolitan Museum. She tries to get them to look at her bus stop stuff, tells them she's not a still-life artist; the scissors piece was an exercise for a class. They do not want to look. They like the scissors. Sam cannot remember, looking at the small canvas, what it felt like to paint it, what inspired her. She has a sick feeling that she hadn't painted it at all, that this is some kind of mistake. She hunts for her name and can't find it, but sells it to them anyway for a lot of money. The dream doesn't disclose the amount, but Sam knows she can live a long time on the check.

She is sleeping, thinking about art and about Adam and about what comes next. The small table near the fireplace holds a photograph of Adam and Aaron. They are standing by a basketball hoop, young and sweaty. The ball is in Adam's hand, held close to his hip. It is easy to tell they are twins, and yet, Sam knows Adam. They are identical. They are mirror physical images. Aaron is dead. Adam wants to marry her. He wants to have children. Sam remembers every detail of the photograph in her dream. She is having a baby. She has the photograph in the hospital. She is trying to tell the two brothers apart and wants to show the father his new child. She holds the frame up. A newborn wriggles on top of her stomach. See daddy. No, wait. Which one is he? There is panic now; she runs the treadmill kind of running one does in a nightmare because she cannot tell which one is Adam. She doesn't know the baby's father. She doesn't know what to do.

Suddenly, on the shelf, the wooden mallard pointed at the lake ruffles its feathers. He turns to her, blinks his eyes, and flies out through the plate-glass window. A clean slice without sound, and the glass closes around the bird like a skin of water. Sam watches it go. She keeps her eyes low on the horizon until it is out of sight. Then she studies the space left on the shelf. The hole left in a flock of birds.

## 23

I t was finally sweatshirt weather. Sam chained her bike to the fence near the doughnut shop and kicked the mud and slush from the spokes. In a booth by the front window, she ate a doughnut and tore little chunks from the rim of her Styrofoam coffee cup. The dirty snow was melting. One could see people's faces again; the mufflers and hats packed away. Sam looked at her notebook and calendar, trying to find a date for a show. A goal.

Rexel slid into the booth across from Sam. "You going to buy me a doughnut?" His face was without emotion.

"Sure. I can manage that. Where have you been? I haven't seen you in a long time."

"I want a powdered and a milk. I'll pay you back."

Sam shrugged and walked back to the counter.

The two sat for a while without talking. Rexel pulled his hooded sweatshirt off. "You're quiet. I ain't seen you quiet before. Somebody steal your dog?"

"God, you are a smart mouth sometimes. It's a wonder I like you, you know it?" Sam's voice was harsh, but softened by the end of the sentence. "Alex is fine; I'm fine. Life sucks. How about you?"

"Life sucks. I've been trying to tell you that, but you're pretty slow. Finally got it, huh?" Rexel pushed powdered sugar around the table with his fingers. "So, what made you figure it out?"

"Let's see, Dr. Freud. What's first? Remember Leah? She's drying out in a treatment center. She drank too much and got herself all banged up in a car accident right in front of my house. And now I'm the enemy. We haven't talked in weeks. I'm too cheerful for her." Sam looked out the window at the empty street. "Don't drink when you grow up, Rexel. It's bad news."

"You don't drink?"

"Some."

"Shit." Rexel got up, pulled on his sweatshirt, and walked outside. Sam followed him and caught up as he turned the corner. The wind was biting, and it felt like more snow. He pulled the sweatshirt hood over his head. Tears rolled down his cheeks.

"What's wrong?" Sam asked, pushing her hands into her pockets. "Rexel. Stop. What is it?"

"You don't get it, do you? You got answers for everything but your own questions." He kept walking. "I ain't gonna feel sorry for you."

The sidewalk was littered with old cans and paper, faded from the winter elements.

"It's worse everywhere. I mean, you got it easy."

"Now wait," Sam said. "Don't judge my life if you don't mind. I just said I was in a rotten mood, okay? Let's drop it."

They walked into the park, reached the swings, and Sam sat down. Rexel stood near her, looking disgusted. "So I suppose you want to act dumb, like a kid, and it's supposed to be okay."

"So what if I do? What's it to you, anyway?"

Rexel leaned against the support pole. "My mom's dead. I went to her funeral four days ago, and now she's dead for good." His voice was forceful and steady. He looked away and then back at Sam. "But I still gotta stay here. I gotta keep living." His voice broke.

Sam's throat tightened in that familiar feeling of panic. She only saw his mother's death in relation to her. She'd been carrying on about her problems, and someone else's were more serious. It was embarrassing. She didn't grasp the death completely. The fresh turned earth. The flowers. All that was unfamiliar. Rexel's grief was a foreign substance in her mouth. His mother was never real to her. She ignored his life. They talked about the world and never got around to the anything real. She didn't know why. At that moment, she didn't know what Rexel was to her. Who was this young boy? Why were they friends? Why did she assume it was okay? "Rexel. I'm… I'm sorry."

He kicked at the icy remnant of a snowdrift. "Yeah, I guess you are. I've been getting used to it for a while."

"What happened? I never knew."

"You didn't ask."

"Right."

"She was real sick."

The simple answer reminded Sam of his age. The poignant cut of sophistication with innocent pain reminded her she was not a part of his life. Not really.

Rexel walked away and turned back. "It's like that. People just leave. You can't make it different. You just got to keep waking up and going to sleep. And waiting… I gotta go."

"Are you going to stay with your aunt?"

"Where else?" he said. "See you around."

## 24

S am sat in the middle of the kitchen floor, opened cans of Play Dough scattered around; a bottle of wine by her side. Four or five small animals stood around her on weak legs. She didn't look up from the blue and yellow dough figure in her hands until Adam cleared his throat.

"Adam! Hello!" Her voice was too loud. "I got a problem. This horse is sick. One leg seems to be too short. You're a vet. You can fix it, can't you? I've been trying like hell, but it just won't cooperate and I got a pig..." She looked around her at the crude animals on the floor. "Here he is. This guy has something wrong with his head. Brain damage. Yup. That's it. Hey, I guess he had a car accident too. Got anything for brain damage, doc? This is Wilber. Ever read Charlotte's Web? God, that was some spider. She saved Wilber's life, you know. Just like that." Sam emptied the bottle into her mouth.

Adam took off his jacket and sat down on the floor near her.

"She wove this web, and it said some damn thing about the pig. I don't remember, but it impressed everybody enough to keep from making him into pork chops. What are you doing here, anyway?"

"I got your message."

"What message? Oh, you mean about Leah? She's dead." Sam's voice lowered. "She got in another car and drove right out of her life." Sam's voice cracked as tears dripped off her chin. "That bitch. She left and didn't even tell me goodbye. Now what kind of friend is that, huh? I mean, we had a few problems, but what kind of friend is that?"

Adam got up and kissed her on the forehead. "I'm sorry. I am."

Sam struggled, stood up, and staggered to the cupboard for another bottle of wine.

"I think you've had enough, Sam." Adam poured some water into a teapot.

"Don't you dare tell me when I've had enough of anything." Sam glared at him. "I'm not driving anywhere. Leah's my designated driver tonight." Sam laughed, her voice crawling into hysterics. "Leah and I used to laugh at most anything." She laughed, wiping tears from her cheeks with the back of her hand. "We drew comic strips of our lives, and let me tell you, they were pretty funny. But she lost the knack."

She walked into the living room and sat down on the futon. "There's got to be something funny in all this, doesn't there? They always say I laughed until I cried. Well, I do things the other way around. Did I ever tell you about my folks? Real jokers, they are. I mean, they'd beat each other around and then cover up the bruises with makeup for the Christmas card photo. That's pretty funny, Adam. Don't you get it? The joke, I mean." Sam paused. "Once my mom sent a new crystal lamp across the living room and it hit our baby grand, scratching it to hell. Lamp was history. Anyway, she and Dad stopped yelling and there was this pause. Mom said, 'Now, where was I?' They both laughed. Tears rolled down their faces. I was fourteen. I remember it was the same time Leah's dad moved out."

Adam went into the bathroom. Sam heard the bath water running.

"Oh, God," she said. "Not another damn bath. What's with you anyway, Mr. Clean? Why are you always trying to wash me off?"

Adam stood in the doorway, smiling. "I guess I've got a fetish for soaping your back."

"I don't blame you." Sam stretched out on the futon.

"It's a damn fine back." She mumbled something and fell asleep, wavy brown hair across her wet face.

A fire engine wailed in the distance. Adam fed the dog and put Sam's menagerie of colorful animals on the kitchen table. He held a small lump of the soft blue clay in his hands, rolling it into a smooth ball.

## 25

"When I heard, I took off into the hills for two days without food or equipment. I just wandered around." Adam pulled a second bagel out of the sack. "I felt cold and hungry and sad. I couldn't run away from it, but I sure tried."

Sam sat in a robe, her hair up in a towel. "Did you follow the war in the papers? Did you know what it was like for him over there?"

"Sure, I followed it, but there wasn't that much written then. Newspapers. TV death counts. I had no idea how the humidity made your clothes stick to you. And the mold and the bugs. The fear. I've read a lot since then; I understand better now how afraid he must have been. Those three months probably felt like a long nightmare or one short one. I don't know. I do know he didn't have time to think about his death when it happened. The explosion killed him instantly. That war fragmented everything. Bodies, lives, battles; everything arrived in a blurred heap over the associated press wire. Aaron's last letter reached me after his death. 'Study hard and don't forget me on the Eve of Destruction.'"

Sam stood up and paced the kitchen. "We're there aren't we? You remember my little friend, Rexel? He always said that. We were on the verge of the end, and it was like it was a mistake we were still here at all. Now his mom died of cancer, and all it does is confirm his belief. So what's the point?"

"I like to think I've made sense of it for myself, but I can't answer it for you. You're on your own."

Sam sat down. "I'm supposed to go to a funeral tomorrow for my best friend, and I don't know what happened, Adam. I don't know how to go to funerals; I've only been to my Gran's, and I wasn't very good at it back then. I guess I'm not very strong."

"It's not a question of strength. It seems to be it's more how you react to the world. All I advise is that you go straight. Feel this thing head on, Sam. It'll save you lots of time and pain later on. Go ahead and feel it. Booze was Leah's camouflage, and it didn't work for her. It won't do you much good either. I'd offer to go along, but that's not my place. I can't be pushing my way into your life right now. It doesn't work, and it isn't worth it. I love you. You know that. I want a chance to love you more, but from here on it's all guesswork. You need to figure out what you want from this. From me. And I don't think now is the time to expect answers. Just live through the next few days." Adam's voice broke. "Tell your friend goodbye. Have a long talk. Get lost in the woods; I don't know. I do know I needed to spend some time next to Aaron's soul. Close to the place in him that started from the same cells I did. Curled up next to the memories of our life together... It was the hardest, most painful week of my life, and nobody could do anything to make it better."

Sam wanted a drink. A heavy glass of amber whiskey. No ice. Just a heavy glass weighing down her arm. Liquid to swirl and smell and swim in. Her first impulse was to drink. Unbelievable. She looked at her hands. They were dry and cracked. Shaking. Tired and torn. She sat back and closed her eyes.

After Adam left, she pulled on a sweatshirt and stocking cap and got her bike out. It was a misty spring day. Sam curled down over her handlebars and watched the slushy bike path in front of her. Lake Calhoun was gray and full of waves. A strong wind stung her face. Her hair was damp from the mist.

Gran had always had answers. After Sam spent her seventh-grade year with her, Gran was the person she could always turn to. She would sit in her kitchen in her housedress and wool slippers and explain why people like her parents always fought: how they weren't suited for each other, why she thought they stayed together, why Sam always got the raw end of the deal. Then she would tell Sam that she needed to understand her parents. She needed to understand that they were human, and sometimes loving them was enough. Sometimes it wasn't. And this time the blowup hadn't been about her staying out late, or not cleaning her room, or not helping at the store. This time, it wasn't about her at all; it was about life and living, and how hard her parents seemed to find it sometimes.

After sitting in Gran's kitchen and listening with her grown up ears, Sam could ride her bike home again. She could go home and walk in smiling, hoping her parents were at the store, hoping, if they were home, they would smile back. Hoping, most of all, that she could go to her bedroom and sit at the window that looked down on the river and think about Huckleberry Finn or the Swiss Family Robinson and pretend her bedroom was a desert island, a quiet, sandy place where she could make her own way.

## 26

The morning was full of sound. Birds filled the budding trees. Sam and Adam sat on the back steps of her place looking out over the fenced backyard. Alex played underneath a twisted old oak. "Aaron and I used to have a treehouse." Adam stared up at the towering tree. "We'd spend every Saturday morning up there planning our attack on the neighbor's place. We didn't like Terry Olson much, so we kept doing rotten things to him, like breaking leaf bags all over his yard or throwing toilet paper in his trees in the middle of the night. We'd camp in the backyard and sneak out. Long white tissue tales hung up there until the next rain."

"Delinquents." Sam ran her fingers through the hair at the base of Adam's neck and kissed him on the top of the head.

"Terrance Matthew. That's what his mother always

called him. 'Terrance Matthew, you need to do your homework now. Terrance Matthew, please get out of that treehouse and come home this instant.' He still played with us, even though he knew we were the ones doing all the damage."

"Now, is that typical boy play or what?" Sam asked. "I remember nothing like that myself. We played Barbie dolls. If you didn't like someone, you didn't invite them over when everyone was playing high school prom."

"Aaron was the instigator. His first letter from Vietnam talked about our treehouse. He thought the observation towers they built were pretty similar. 'Looking for Charlie,' he said. That was pretty weird. There was no collective enemy. Just this one guy named Charlie. His letters were full of things like 'We've been on a thirty-six hour alert. Old Charlie is supposed to mortar us. We have sixteen Chinook choppers in and he is trying for them. He blew up the road between here and Saigon Sunday morning." Adam shook his head. "He'd tell about how Charlie had blown up the road in four places nearby. How he got Ben Hai air base. The first couple of letters were full of what 'Charlie' was doing. Nothing about my brother. Nothing about being afraid. That came later."

"What could you say?" Sam sat up straight and squinted up at the open sky. "I mean, what could you write to him? God."

"I told him about medical school, about my tennis game, about how the fish weren't biting, and we'd have to get some fishing in when he got home. How we'd have to play chess and get drunk and tell stories. He wrote back and said he was doing all that at night. Playing chess, sometimes in the dark. Playing chess, swearing, drinking, and telling stories. Telling about high school football games so you wouldn't hear Charlie out in the jungle. So you wouldn't hear Charlie all around you, breathing down your neck." Adam blinked several times. "When I'd envision him sitting there in the mud and mosquitos, I'd see myself. I mean, he looked just like me. Was me, sort of, you know? There I'd be, in the middle of campus, reading about this nightmare. And I'd be awake. And I'd want to tell him, hey, Aaron, climb the ladder and get your butt up in this treehouse, It's safe up here, man! It's quiet, and it's safe, and we can see for miles."

The morning was warming, and it smelled like wet earth. Tulips lined the steps next to where they sat. Purple and yellow cups of color. Sparrows and robins in the trees. Small wings busying themselves with spring nests. Small hearts beating like crazy.

## 27

The highway followed the river as Sam drove southeast out of Red Wing. It was warm for late April. She pushed a button that lowered the two front windows. It was a plush car. The wind grabbed a strand of her hair and sucked it out of the window. Nothing seemed familiar anymore: driving Adam's BMW, driving away from her life, even if it was only for a few days. Sam felt like sections of her past were blowing away, flying off on the warm wind like newspapers on the hood of a speeding car.

The car's leather seats smelled like money. Her parents sold the occasional leather sofa to some business office downtown that wanted to impress people. Put a full grain leather sofa in an office, and you'd get respect. Could she marry Adam? It was possible, Sam thought, but how do I keep it from getting boring? How do I keep him from going to bars, to dinner, to the theater with other women? How do I stay happy?

Sam pulled into a small two pump gas station. Marigolds grew next to the door. A cat was asleep on the seat of an old bicycle. An older man in overalls walked up to the window.

"Fill it up, please." Sam stayed in the car. He washed the windshield, looking at her the whole time. "You want the oil checked?"

"I don't know." Sam braided her hair with one hand.

The man chuckled. "You just buy a new one when it runs low?"

Sam laughed and got out of the car, looking it over as if she'd never seen it before. "That's funny, I was driving an old VW Bug when I left Minneapolis. How did I get into this thing?"

The attendant took off his Twins baseball cap and scratched his thinning hair. "Do tell. And I suppose you want to use a credit card to pay?"

Sam pulled a crumpled twenty out of her pocket. "I hope I get some back because I need to get some lunch."

The man returned with the change, still smiling. "Wonderful restaurant in Lake City. Rotten coffee, though. Try their homemade pie. All but the cherry. They use canned ones. Good apple and banana cream. Traveling far?"

"However far my oil takes me, thanks." Sam smiled

and got back in the car. She pulled out of the station, trying to memorize the scene. The trip was worth this. You don't see places like this in the city, she thought. She felt better having spoken to someone she didn't know. She'd played a little. Made a couple jokes. It helped; it always helped.

The road stretched out ahead of her. Sam grew used to the steering wheel, the smooth lull of the highway.

Marry Adam? Have a baby? Here she was, driving a car she'd have put down as decadent a year before, and she still did. It seemed impossible, not worrying about money, being able to do some things she wanted, being in love. She loved him, but that was the easy part; it was the rest of her life that looked too scary to consider. She needed a weekend. She felt like a paper doll, with the tabs all torn off her dress and her neck worn. In need of support. Scotch tape. Sleep. She needed time.

It was a long day. When the light faded, Sam walked along the streets of downtown Wabasha, thinking about Rexel, circling blocks near his home and counting footsteps. How he kept his life in safe, controlled increments, taking it step by step. She thought about being sixteen and riding around downtown St. Cloud with Leah, with boys. Dating, driving the loop, and then stopping in the city park by the river and making out. There was one boy she thought she loved. He was the only one she would have said yes to—she would have had sex then, with him, despite the risks. She would have, but he never asked.

She thought about growing up. College. London. Putting her life together like a puzzle. Traveling in Europe, she began to feel good about herself when she was on her own for the first time with no family baggage. She was in control. From the wealth of art in Florence to the sacred history of the Acropolis, Samantha Ellings felt her heart beat for the very first time.

In the old hotel in town, Sam sat in an oversized T-shirt. She picked up the phone and called Allison in San Francisco. "I'm sitting on an old brass bed in this little town on the river. I don't know why I'm here, but I'm here. I drove Adam's BMW."

"He's not with you?"

"No. That was the deal. He offered to take me on a weekend vacation. Said we'd drive down the river. I took him up on the car and on the drive."

"How are you?"

"Good. Bad. Okay. I don't know."

"So what's up? Listen, I heard about Leah. I'm sorry."

"You never even called. You knew, and you didn't call me?"

"Sam, it's not like we speak on the phone much. I didn't know if you'd want to talk to me. You could have called too, you know."

"I am. I'm calling now."

"So talk to me."

After the conversation, Sam sat at the window. Her room looked out over a black tar roof down onto the street. She felt like a child when she talked to her sister. Why didn't I tell her I was afraid of this relationship? she wondered. Is it all right to be afraid? I could have told her I was still having the dream. I am so tired, but if I go to sleep, there may be soldiers floating on the river again. Young men who look like Adam, rising and failing in the nightmare waters, young men in uniforms. Lily pads. Sisters on the beach. Maybe tonight one sister will kiss a boy in uniform. The other sister will hide behind a tree. Watching. Hiding and watching.

## 28

"It's not only that I want to be a father. I'm thirty-two years old. I'm ready to settle down. I could have gotten married before, but I never chose to until now. Is that a crime? What are you afraid of, Sam?"

"Where would you like me to start?"

"Anywhere. I need to know if it's me. I mean, are you afraid of getting married, or of marrying me?"

"Yes."

Adam waited, still looking at Sam.

"I feel like I'm from another planet, Adam. You have money and a reputation for your work. You're secure. And where do I come into that? I don't even know what I want to do with my life. I love my work, but when backed against the fence, I haven't followed up on anything. Like I don't even have goals. Maybe I don't believe I'm an artist. I guess I need to find out."

"But why does that have to be separate from me? Why do you see everything as for or against?"

"I don't know." Sam turned toward the lake. "Everything has sides, Adam. If I'm ever going to marry you, I have to be on your side."

"What about me being on yours? For an independent woman, you keep putting everything into the context of submitting to me, to my lifestyle. I've never asked for that. If things change, we change them together. It's not the things that are different about us that stand out for me. It's the things we both enjoy. The world we live in together."

Sam hugged Adam, sliding the car keys into the back pocket of his jeans. "Thanks for the loan. It felt good to get out of the city." She turned toward the house. "I have to go."

"Sam, let me drive you home."

"Not this time. Thanks. I'll catch a bus. Excellent material on buses." Sam smiled, her shoulders drooping as if tired. She raised her eyebrows. "I'll call you."

Adam ran his fingers through his hair. "I can't stand this, you know. Call me. Think seriously about us, Sam. I want some commitment; I need it. I honestly don't know anymore if you can give me that. Sometimes I can't even see you when you're standing right in front of me. I swear you're great at building walls." He paused. "I'd like to get on with our lives. I was thinking of marriage or living together or whatever. Together." He smiled and shook his head. "You know, I was even thinking about building a studio on the west end of the house. Just … you know … if you liked the idea."

Sam shook her head. "Don't try so hard, Adam. I feel you are pushing me."

"I guess I'm jumping ahead here, but I need to know where you stand. My feelings count on this thing, too."

Sam backed away, hands in the pockets of her jeans. Lake Minnetonka pulled blue from the sky. Bright, incredible blue. The sand. The leaves. Everything was gorgeous. Landscaped. Paid for. She felt the scene fading alarmingly fast as the late afternoon light shadowed Adam's hopeful smile.

## 29

Rexel was outside the music store, sitting on a mountain bike, leaning against the brick wall with one arm. Sam saw him before he saw her. Another boy on a bike balanced near him. They were joking about something. "Fox," the other kid said as Sam walked up.

"Sam!" Rexel looked surprised, then pleased. He recovered quickly. Covered it.

"Hi, Rexel. Long time. What are you up to?"

"This is Robert." Rexel fiddled with the hand brakes, looking down at his peddles. An adolescent. It struck Sam. This was an adolescent with a friend. Rexel was acting like any kid. Half smile. Popping wheelies.

"Hi." She smiled at the boy. Red hair. Braces. She turned back to Rexel. "So how's it going?"

"Okay. You?"

She shrugged. "Can't complain. Nice bike."

"I got a paper route."

"Cool." Sam paused. "So things are okay?"

"Yeah." Rexel pulled a baseball cap out of his back pocket and put it on. "All right." He squinted into the sun.

"I'm glad." Sam could sense his discomfort. She was getting too close. The rules were different now. A new distance limit. Friends his age. The world between them. "Take it easy, okay? It was nice to see you." She headed down the block toward Netty's high-rise.

Rexel nodded. As Sam turned the corner, she heard his friend. "Who's the fox? How do you know her?"

Sam smiled. She wanted to hear Rexel's reply. She missed him. Things happen, she thought. People come and go and leave holes, but this time she could see light through the hole. She could definitely see the sunshine.

## 30

"Bart said I could have more hours if I wanted to work on the bookkeeping stuff. I don't know. Summer's coming up." Sam released the right brake and pushed Netty's wheelchair out of the room and down the hall. "I'm not sure I want to work forty hours, but I could use the money. I could stand a couple more long weekend vacations like last weekend. That old hotel was great. Homemade bread and jelly. Tea. It reminded me of England and the bread and breakfasts I used to go to." Sam reached a bench and sat down in the sunshine next to Netty's. She put her hand on the old woman's thin, freckled arm. It felt like Gran's arm: cool and pale with a grip that would shock any politician.

"Well, what is it, Sam? I know it's not Leah. At least not only Leah."

"I don't know, Netty. When I was in college, we did

this experiment with white rats. You know, the maze stuff. My rat never wanted to go through the maze to get the food. She didn't even try. She'd stand right where I put her down and shake—petrified. My lab partner decided she was slow. His rat ran through the maze in record time, of course. In my final paper, I said my rat was just afraid of going on. Where she'd been hadn't been that great, and she didn't know if the reward was worth finding out what was ahead. I said I thought we needed to do experiments on rats that weren't in a hurry to get somewhere and we might learn something."

A couple of joggers ran past, legs moving together like clockwork. Netty remained quiet.

"I'm not in a hurry either. Adam wants to get married. He's great. I love him, but he wants to tie it all up in a neat package and take care of me. Then I can have kids and take care of them and… " Sam looked at Netty. "I don't know how to do any of this. I'm not giving him credit. No man has ever treated me with such kindness and respect. I mean, he isn't smothering me; he wouldn't dominate me, I don't think, but he wants something. That's for damn sure, and I don't know what I'm supposed to do.

Netty smiled. "In 1936 Elroy and I moved to St. Cloud from Bismark. He wanted to farm with his brother. We got a tiny clapboard house with a sagging front porch and two gorgeous apple trees on the west end. After we'd already moved, I started asking myself if it was what I wanted. How I felt about it. Of course, I never discussed it with Elroy. Instead, I canned apples until I couldn't see straight and made apple butter and apple pie and cider by the gallon. The kitchen steam and summer sweat baked into my skin, and I finally knew where I wanted my life to be." Netty pulled her sweater over her shoulders. "I peeled a lot of apples before I figured that one out."

Sam squinted into the sun. "Some help you are."

Netty played with the bun at the nape of her neck. "I can give you a tasty recipe for apple butter."

## 31

Dear Allison,

Have you ever thought about raising a family? I mean babies and everything? Have you and Joe ever talked about children? Do you want to have them? Would you still work? Do you think you would be a good…

DEAR ALLISON,

Hello. How are you? How's Joe? I hope things are going well.

I'm writing because I think I might be in love. Well, I am in love. I mean, I love Adam, but I don't know what I plan to do about it. I don't know if I love him enough. How does anybody know?

I've never felt this way before. I'm learning that I'm pretty shaky in this category, though. Trust hasn't been a real staple in my life. Have you ever thought about having a baby? Have you...

DEAR ALLISON,

I finally had that talk with Adam. About the future and all that. He wants one. All wrapped up tidy with little gold wedding rings and his and hers towels. But do you want to know a secret? I think I might want that too; I'm not sure. I mean, what's wrong with it? Why do I keep fighting it? Did you? With Joe, I mean?

I think I've been fighting things all along, but I don't know why I've been fighting it. God, every time I write to you, I convince myself that I need a shrink.

DEAR ALLISON,

I miss Leah. Sometimes I can't believe...

DEAR ALLISON,

Hello. Here I sit again, big sister, trying to figure out my life by writing to you on blue-lined. Adam wants to marry me. I love him, but I am not sure I love him enough. Our lives are so different. He wants to have children. Someday I want to too, I think. As long as I wouldn't end up yelling at them and throwing things. I want to be a good parent. I want my kids to feel safe; you know?

Adam lives in this unbelievable house on an incredible lake. He wants to build a studio for me. I would live in this gorgeous house overlooking the lake. I don't know if I can feel comfortable in such a rich environment.

It isn't Adam. Adam isn't the problem. He is wonderful and kind and intelligent. Is it his money that I can't get used to? I don't know.

Dumb argument. Skip it. It isn't all that easy. It's not one thing. Adam is willing to work all this out. He says he understands more about me than I tell him, that some injuries speak from the body instead of from the mouth, and I'm holding in some kind of pain and building walls around it. He could be right. I need to figure out what those walls are. I don't know if I'm ready to connect with someone else when I still need to put myself together.

I don't deserve him. It all seems so easy, Allison. He cares about me. He encourages me and has patience like no person I have ever known. I have never had anyone else make my happiness for me, and I'm not good at enjoying it. But hell, why don't I deserve a little happiness? When is it my turn?

Go out and ask the ocean for me, will you? Throw in a bottle and tell me if it sinks.

Love,

Sam

## 32

S am was thinking about the oboe. She sat tossing
sticks across the yard for her dog. Tossing sticks
to Alex and thinking about throwing the oboe
into the Mississippi river. The year she started to grow
up. That horn never made it to New Orleans, she thought,
but I spent a lot of time hoping it would. An oboe in jazz
town. Being twelve years old wasn't easy, but then,
neither was this stuff.

It was the kind of day when the blue was so bold it
seemed to open the sky and make room for more space
between trees and tall buildings. "I want to do my art,"
she said aloud to Alex, to no one in particular. "I need to
draw, and paint, and feel good again. There's no river for
miles; I should be able to manage some peace of mind,
shouldn't I?"

The comment surprised her. The river, the nightmares

and floating bodies, the oboe. Did that long dock from her childhood reach this far? "I am forever throwing things into the water, Alex." Sam shook her head. "Out of control." She put the dog in the house, changed her T-shirt and headed to the corner bus. Adam would be home.

Sam felt a little shaky sitting on the vinyl seat. She knew she had something to say. Articulating it was another matter. It always had been. How she felt and what she said were separate actions in her life. Today, there wasn't time to build that protective safety hatch for escape.

Did she deserve to be happy or not? Wasn't it that simple? All her life, all the men she'd wanted to love, all the chances she'd taken, left her at night with a stereo and a skylight in the ceiling, where all she could see were the icy stars.

Adam was offering something different. Why did she view it as charity? Sam glanced at an older woman near the back of the bus. It looked like Gran in her blue cotton housedress. "Don't you think you deserve to be happy?" Gran would have whispered, her fingers tucking stray hairs back into her bun. It was as if she was there on the bus, and suddenly everyone had something to say to Sam.

Rexel was next to her, near the skin of reality, near the place Sam could touch. "And what about love, Sam? Feeling good? This fantastic world you keep talking about. The one that will be around for a while." Sam could hear his voice in her head, could see his intense eyes.

And if Gary were there, perhaps driving the bus, he would shout at her in the rearview mirror. "Is your work good enough? Is that what you're worried about? Would you ever devote full time to it, if you could? Come on, lady. We want answers."

Sam wondered if she could devote full time to anything. She looked around the bus for a blonde woman. A Leah. The mirror image that might lend one more clue, but she wasn't there. Like the graves in *Our Town*, some folks slept through the act or refused to talk.

Sam touched the back of the seat in front of her and looked at her hand, looked at the fingernails and skin. Finding clues. Was she talented enough to make it as an artist? She was afraid to find out.

"Sam," Gran said from the backseat, from the years and years between them. "It's not your fault. We can deal with this."

She thought about Leah. In high school, Sam would drag her to the art room to show her a new project. To get approval. She wanted approval so she could spend her life doing this kind of art. Feeling alive. Leah always said the right thing, always gave permission to seek happiness. Sam seemed to need permission.

Happiness. That elusive bird bobbing in the water with the decoys, its eyes looking like the painted wooden eyes of its sisters. Maybe it was all right to get confused, to lose control. Sam remembered the good times as a kid. The times she curled in her father's lap and watched the World Series. The time the family vacationed in the Black Hills and posed by the huge dinosaur models. Her mother combing her hair with her fingers. Her mother touching her shoulder. Allison sneaking popcorn into their room late at night and reading Nancy Drew mysteries aloud. And later, reading books Sam didn't understand, but reading anyway, aloud in the dark with a flashlight, reading to her.

Sam got off the bus and walked to Adam's house. She rang the bell, not rehearsing a line, thinking only about cement dinosaur statues and baseball games.

Adam stood at the door. Surprise, and then a smile. "Sam. Hello."

"Hi." She smiled and took a deep breath. "May I come in?"

# ACKNOWLEDGMENTS

Chapters six and ten from this book were previously published as short stories "White Paint" and "Storm" in my short story collection, *Anxiety in the Wilderness.*

# THANK YOU

Thank you to my family and friends who read *Perfume River* before it was published and reassured me that the story was ready to be told: Bob, Colleen x 2, Hanna, Eunice, Jackie, Jean, Jeff, Kim, Paris, Rick, Sinead, Tammy, and Victoria.

# ABOUT THE AUTHOR

Kathleen Patrick is a poet and fiction writer who grew up on the prairies of the Midwest, riding horses, jumping rope, hula hooping, and writing poetry. Her bestselling book, *Airmail: A Story of War in Poems*, centers on her family's experience with wars, from the Vietnam War to the present. *Mercy*, her first novel, is a coming-of-age story set in 1970 on the plains of South Dakota. *Anxiety in the Wilderness* is her first collection of short stories. *Perfume River,* a novel for adults, is her fourth book.

# FREE SHORT STORY!

Sign up for my mailing list at the address below and get a free short story! "Anxiety in the Wilderness" is the title story from my recent collection of short stories by the same title.

https://patrickpoetry.com/

## ALSO BY KATHLEEN PATRICK

Airmail: A Story of War in Poems

Mercy

Anxiety in the Wilderness

Perfume River

# WORDS AND REVIEWS

Airmail: A Story of War in Poems

"I read it in one sitting and thoroughly enjoyed (if that's the right word) every poem." — Tim O'Brien, author of *The Things They Carried*

*"Airmail: A Story of War in Poems*…is a great example of how letters and conversations can be turned into stunning poetry. Patrick shares the words and thoughts of seven uncles who served in the military, five of them in Southeast Asia during the American war in Vietnam. …It's always cool to see letters sent home from war turned into poems. They become letters from America sent back to America. Kathleen Patrick shows us what it can look like when it's done poetically and done right." — Bill McCloud, The VVA Veteran magazine

"Love the voice and reading pace. It's great, and the content is amazing. I am a Vietnam vet and I can relate 100%. Thanks for taking the time to do this project." — J.I.

"Some very strong work here, grounded in correspondence that Kathleen had with her uncles while they served in Vietnam, and also in their correspondence with their parents, subsequent interviews, etc. An amazing piece of work. This is the best war

lit I have read since *The Things they Carried* by Tim O'Brien."
— P.L.

"A story that stays with you. I read a lot of historical fiction surrounding WWI and II, but this collection of poems highlighting the perspectives of a family living through Vietnam was just as beautiful. Reading poetry framed as letters by young men wanting to serve and the loved ones they left behind was powerfully written and even more powerful in the things that were left unsaid. This is a collection that should be read slowly, absorbing the words from each letter. — A. C.

"Wow…Honestly, I don't read a lot of poetry and didn't think I would like it. However, I loved it; it sucked me right in, and I thought it was beautifully done." — L.M.

"This collection distills so much family history into consumable little poems that will leave you wrecked in the best possible way. A beautiful read." — H.C.

*"Airmail: A Story of War in Poems* is a book about going off to war, a book about coming back home, and a book about those who are left behind." — Kathleen Patrick

Mercy

"*Mercy* is a phenomenal young adult coming of age story that will capture the hearts of readers of all ages!"—K.C.

"*Mercy* is a story of adolescence, but adults would love it as well. It explores the emotional turbulence inherent in dysfunctional families and what it takes to move from dysfunction to love to mercy. Any book that can make me cry and laugh out loud is a winner. *Mercy* is a winner!"—J.C.

"A coming of age, found family, young adult novel. A heartwarming story about a twelve-year-old girl named Sadie who finds the family she always craved in her uncle on a farm. After Sadie's mother struggles with gambling addiction after her father's departure, Sadie has a life of instability and worry. Great short read. The only thing I have to say bad about the story is that it simply isn't long enough!"—K.F.

"Mercy was just a great story and a breath of fresh air!" — L.P.

"Mercy is a story about compassion and kindness. It celebrates the idea families can come in all shapes and sizes and consists of people who support one another, even when it isn't easy. It is a story that reverberates with the basic human need to be loved."—Kathleen Patrick

## Anxiety in the Wilderness

"A book of short stories that can only be described as bittersweet. Some parts defiantly pulled at my heartstrings. The author herself said the book was written over a long time period. This comes across in the different scenarios in which the characters are involved in. Each a little exceptional tale of it's own. I especially liked the crossover of characters. I am now patiently waiting for a full novel set in the Iowa wilderness!" —K. F., Goodreads review

"The poetic language of the stories lends a warmth to the storytelling that helps to bring the characters to life. Each story describes a different human worry or anxiety that we all may have experienced at some point in our lives; therefore, each story is relatable in its own way....Short stories are a disappearing art form, and Patrick demonstrates why we should keep them around. There is no grandiosity of language that detracts from the storyline or from the artful character descriptions. Characters navigate their way through their predicaments one day at a time. The poignant vignettes showcase the rawness of various human emotions, much like a snapshot of an expert photographer. " —B. M., Goodreads Review

"I loved this book! From beginning to end the characters smack of realism and you can see people you know or yourself in them. I wish it were the first book I a series of ten — because I wanted more!"

Perfume River

"The characters are well drawn, and the story is both touching and humorous. Worth the read!" E.S.

"Patrick's prose is smooth, even, and consistent. As with her other work, her use of words is sparse and succinct leaving the reader to indulge in their own imaginings of the space and events. The pauses and silences are evocative." J.S.

"Absolutely loved the main character! Great read!" K. K.

"I enjoy Kathleen Patrick's concise descriptive abilities sprinkled with emotional and intellectual truths." CT

"It is a beautifully written novel with deep feelings. It is the kind of book that wins prizes." E.S.